D1229932

Down
in
Texas

Down in Texas

Delilah Devlin

APHRODISIA

KENSINGTON PUBLISHING CORP.

APHRODISIA BOOKS are published by

Kensington Publishing Corp.
850 Third Avenue
New York, NY 10022

Copyright © 2008 by Delilah Devlin

All rights reserved. No part of this book may be reproduced in any form or by any means without the prior written consent of the Publisher, excepting brief quotes used in reviews.

Special book excerpts or customized printings can also be created to fit specific needs. For details, write or phone the office of the Kensington special sales manager: Kensington Publishing Corp., 850 Third Avenue, New York, NY 10022, attn: Special Sales Department, Phone: 1-800-221-2647.

Aphrodisia and the A logo Reg. U.S. Pat & TM Off.

ISBN-13: 978-1-60751-393-3

Printed in the United States of America

Contents

Wearing His Brand

1

Her daddy had always told her a man's worth wasn't measured by the size of his bank account or the square footage of his house. Rather, it could be seen in the proud set of his shoulders or a gaze that didn't waiver.

Her mama had said a man's strength was in his hands—strong and soothing when an animal or a child needed comfort, hot and wild when a woman needed shaking up.

Looking at Brand now, Lyssa McDonough knew exactly what they'd both meant.

If she had any sense at all she'd turn tail and run. Everything about the man screamed heartbreaker.

Only, she couldn't. Instead she settled her shoulder against the fence post, kept her breaths shallow and even, and pretended she wasn't melting inside.

As long as she could remember, Brand had had that effect on her—long before she had admitted, even to herself, how much he moved her. Today, dressed in a wash-softened chambray shirt that stretched across his broad chest, blue jeans that hugged lean hips, and leather chaps encasing thick thighs, he was the embodiment of any woman's favorite cowboy fantasy.

Once again, she wished that she affected him the same way, that just looking at her made him breathless. The sight she presented him at this moment, however, would never inspire lust.

Covered in dust and sweat, with hair straggling from the confines of its rubber band, she was grimy, bloody, and anything but attractive.

Too far away to read his expression, Lyssa watched how he stood in the stirrups as he topped the hill, head turning to scan the countryside. When his gaze landed on her, his back stiffened, he settled into his saddle, and his boots spurred his horse to bring him fast down the hill.

Things could have turned out worse.

The day might have broken with a cloudless, blue sky and a white-hot sun beating relentlessly on her unprotected face. Early summer in southwest Texas could be ruthless, but thick, gray clouds had gathered, shielding her from the worst of the heat. Still, she was thirsty, and her canteen was deep in the satchel of the horse that had to be halfway back to the ranch house by now.

She might not have worn the industrial-padded bra that was the only thing keeping one nasty barb from tearing the tender flesh of her breast like the other that pierced the back of her shoulder. The pointed barb only pricked, a reminder not to take deeper breaths. Vanity had guided her choice. She'd chosen the thick-cupped bra hoping she'd see him today, hoping he'd finally take a closer look and realize she was more than his best friend's little sister.

More than an obligation he'd accepted.

The promise he'd made was the crux of her problem with Brandon Tynan.

Lyssa dragged away her gaze and readied herself for what she knew was coming. Again, she stretched the toe of her boot toward the wire cutters she'd dropped when she'd first felt the tension in the barbed wire ease and heard it "sing" as it snapped from a post farther down the fence.

The wire had coiled so fast she'd had time only to spit out the bent nails she'd held between her teeth. It had snagged her, pulling her off her feet, and wrapped around her. The merciless wire had trapped her arms against her sides and her shoulder against the post to which she'd been securing new strands of wire to replace the cut ones.

When the barb atop her left breast bit deeper, she gritted her teeth and sagged against the post. Brand would have to get her out of her current coil.

Damn. The man loved rubbing her nose in her mistakes.

Hooves thundered closer. She wiped the pain-filled grimace from her face and turned to meet his steady gaze as he reined in his horse.

Brand slipped from the saddle as soon as Ranger slid to a stop, kicking up a cloud of dust.

Because Lyssa couldn't tilt her head higher as he approached, she watched his booted feet eat the distance between them.

He knelt on one knee beside her and tipped his hat off his head to hang from the stampede string knotted at his throat. His gaze raked her body once before locking with her gaze.

Inwardly she braced herself. His expression was darker than the thunderheads building in the sky above them. "Lyssa, didn't I tell you not to ride the fence alone?"

She blinked at the raw tension in his deep, rumbling voice, and then felt her eyebrows draw together in a fierce scowl. "I've been mending fences all my life. I didn't need any help. This was just pure bad luck."

"We're gonna talk about this, soon as I get you free."

3

"Damn you, Brand." Furious tears burned the back of her eyes, but she blinked them back. "No 'Are you all right? Are you thirsty?' No, you have to start in—"

"Fuck." He scrubbed his deeply tanned face with the back of a leather glove before meeting her gaze again. "Are you okay?"

She sniffed, wishing she could reach up and rub her nose. "Too late."

"I was worried. The hands said you'd been gone a long time. When I found your horse . . ." He took a deep breath, and his gaze slid to the clouds overhead.

Only slightly mollified with his nonapology, she sighed, letting the anger slide away and glaring at the wire doubled around her torso. "Just cut me loose."

"Don't think I can," he said softly.

She shot him an irritated glance. "The cutters are at my feet. . . ." Her voice faded as she stared.

Brand's expression had lost its angry tension. Sure, a muscle flexed along his square jaw, but his dark brown eyes held a tenderness she'd never observed.

Before she had a moment to ponder what it meant, he stood and unbuttoned his shirt, tugging it from the waist of his jeans.

She'd seen his tanned, bared chest before—had drooled over the smattering of black-brown hair that stretched between his small, male nipples and sighed when imagining herself lightly stroking her fingertips along the thick slabs of muscle filling out his masculine chest and shoulders.

Her breath caught, pushing her breast against the barb. Air hissed between her teeth.

He bent quickly. "Don't move, I'm gonna slide this under the wire. Let me know if I hurt you."

Lyssa held her breath as his hand slipped between her breasts and under the wire. Slowly he pressed against the thickly padded material cupping a meager curve, working his way toward the barb, and then he pulled the wire away from her, sliding the bunched shirt under the wire.

Lyssa ground her teeth as the prongs embedded in her shoulder cut deeper.

"I'm hurting you. Where next?"

"Behind my shoulder," she bit out.

Brand crawled over her sprawled legs and circled behind her. "Damn, you're bleeding."

She opened her mouth to deliver her usual caustic "duh" but clamped her mouth shut, not wanting to spoil the tender moment stretching between them. "I'm all right. It just stings."

"I can't pad it. I'll have to cut the wire to get it out."

"Thanks for the warning," she murmured.

He leaned to grab the wire cutters. "I'll make it quick."

"Just do it."

A snip drove the barb deeper. Lyssa squeezed her eyes shut as Brand pulled it out. Two more snips, and he dragged away the rest of the wire before kneeling beside her once again.

Lyssa dropped her head and dragged in deep, trembling breaths. Her shoulder and breast burned like fire, but the ordeal was over now.

A large, broad palm entered her line of vision. "Let's get you home and have a look at that shoulder."

She accepted the hand he extended and almost groaned with relief when another hand gripped her waist to lift her to her feet. She felt weak as a baby, and her legs tingled as blood rushed back into cramped limbs.

"Can you walk?"

Lyssa flashed Brand an incredulous look and shook off the hand around her waist. When the one gripping her hand tightened, she didn't fight him, just let him lead her slowly toward his horse.

"Anyone ever tell you you're as stubborn as an old mule?" he said, reaching for the canteen looped around his saddle horn.

She let go of his hand and accepted the canteen, giving the cap a twist. "You. More times than I can count."

A small, tight smile stretched one side of his mouth as he stared while she upended the canteen and let the water spill into her mouth. She didn't care when it trickled along her cheek and down her neck.

"Slow down," he said. "You'll be sick."

Because he was right, and, more so, because a sudden weariness sapped her strength, she didn't argue. She handed back the canteen and waited while he stowed it and his bloodied shirt in a saddlebag and gathered the tools strewn on the ground.

When he came back to her side, he handed her the hat she'd lost. "Hold this." Then he gripped her waist and lifted her gently over the saddle. He settled her sideways, the horn between her thighs, and then stepped up, sliding into his seat behind her.

She'd never been this close to Brand before. The juncture of his thighs pressed against the side of her hip. If she leaned, her cheek would lie against bare skin.

Suddenly she felt unsettled. Her stomach tightened. She hoped the water she'd drunk wasn't getting ready to rush back up. When his arm gently encircled her waist, she jerked at the intimate touch.

"Rest against me," he said, his voice deepening. "I won't jostle you as much."

Lyssa knew he was probably just being kind as she relaxed against him and fought against her rising excitement. She slid an arm around his waist to hold on as he nudged his horse forward; she noted that she felt no softness, just hard muscle clothed in skin smooth as oiled leather.

Snuggling her cheek against him, she enjoyed the feel of the soft, swirling hairs that furred his chest, and she inhaled the smell of the man who'd filled her head with lustful thoughts since she'd reached puberty.

His scent—plain soap and his unique musk—filled her nostrils, calming her thudding heart. Another deeper inhalation, and she let her body rock in the saddle with his body as he kept his horse at a slow, even gait.

Even though her wounds ached, she was over being sorry that she'd landed in such a mess. She'd wanted him to notice her.

Things could have turned out worse.

Brand gritted his teeth and tried to calm the riot of feelings flooding his body. Every rocking movement made him aware of just what part of his body was rubbing against her slim hip. His cock crowded tighter by the minute against the fly of his jeans.

The way she sat, snuggled up against him, her soft cheek sliding on his skin, her slim fingers clutching his waist . . . he wished he could spur Ranger to race toward the ranch house so he could dump her sweet body on the porch and end the torment.

With one smart-mouth comment, Lyssa could trigger his anger faster than fire licking at dry prairie grass. However, the sight of her mouth tightened with pain had shot an arrow straight through his heart.

Worse, horned toad that he was, the trembling of her full bottom lip—and the tears glittering in her wide, green eyes as he'd cut away the wire—had sent his thoughts straight south.

Not for the first time, he'd wished he could gather her in his arms and soothe away all her worries, ease all her hurts. But he knew where that would lead. One intimate, tender touch, and he'd be a goner, his promise as empty as the wide-open spaces stretching in front of them.

Brand wanted to soothe his own aches while sinking every inch of his cock into Lyssa McDonough's silky depths.

However, Lyssa wasn't a woman he could play with and leave. She was his best friend's sister. Before Mac's reserve unit had been mobilized, he'd extracted Brand's promise to make sure she stayed safe. Watching over the woman didn't include sleeping with her—no matter how tempting her sexy little body was or how much she might want to experiment.

He'd have to be blind not to note how her gaze followed him. How curiosity gleamed in her eyes or colored her cheeks whenever they were together. Over the years, deflecting her interest had become a natural habit.

Brand had learned to use her anger to protect himself from his own growing attraction. He gave her a narrowed glance. "What do you think you were doing, riding alone?"

She stiffened in his arms, eyes flashing.

Brand tightened his grip on her waist, not wanting her to harm herself, all the while acutely aware that his thumb rode the bottom edge of her bra.

"A load of hay's coming. I needed most of the hands to unload the trailer."

"Why didn't you call me?" he growled.

"Who made you my keeper?"

His glare intensified. "Mac did. You know it."

"I don't need a baby-sitter."

"What happened to the fence?"

She bristled with tension, and he suppressed a grim smile. Lyssa was predictable.

"Someone cut it."

"Third time in a month. Don't you think that warrants a little caution?" She stayed silent so long he knew she agreed but was searching for a plausible excuse for today's actions.

"I'm not missing any cattle," she said.

"Maybe they're scoping out the place first. Or maybe it's not rustlers. We're damn close to the border."

Her head tilted back. "You think it might be smugglers?"

"Could be. Reason enough to take precautions."

"I carry a rifle."

"Oh?" he said, letting his gaze slide over her body. "Where's it now?"

Her eyebrows drew into a testy frown. "With my horse."

Brand sighed. "Lyssa, we've got to come to an understanding. You're gonna take my advice."

"Or what?" Lyssa asked, a new, sultry note entering her voice. "What are you gonna do? Spank me?" Her hip wiggled against him.

Shock at her drawled suggestion had him sucking in a deep breath. A vision of Lyssa, her naked body draped over his knees, made his dick pulse. "Would you like that?" he asked softly.

"Maybe I would," she whispered, lowering her eyelids halfway.

His gaze dropped to her mouth as pink lips opened around a gasp.

"I can't believe I just said that. To you."

He narrowed his eyes. "It slipped kinda easy from your lips. Someone else you been teasing, baby girl?"

"I don't tease."

Brand ground his teeth at the solemn promise in her eyes. "Juanita at your house?"

Her head shook, and tendrils of wild, red hair moved around her face. "She's in town doing some shopping."

He swore softly and pointed his horse west.

"Thought you were taking me home."

"I am. My home."

"But we're closer to mine."

"You want Hector or Santiago cleanin' you up?"

Her chin lifted. "I'll manage on my own."

"What about your shoulder?"

Her breath huffed, but a moment later she whispered, "So you're gonna do it?"

The small, feminine smile beginning to curve her lips had him tightening like a bowstring. "I'll tend your wounds; then I'm drivin' you straight home."

"Whatever you say."

"Now you're all agreeable," he grumbled, pretending an irritation that was totally at war with the anticipation building in his body.

"I'm not unreasonable. Makes sense," she said breathlessly. "You tending my wounds. Nothing Mac wouldn't have done."

Shit. If Mac knew the thoughts running through his mind, he'd string him up by his balls. Brand pulled up to the gate between the two properties and leaned down to unlatch it. "Like I said, after we're done, I'm takin' you straight home."

2

Lyssa sat in a ladder-back chair in the kitchen while Brand hunted through the pantry for the first-aid kit. Judging by the amount of noise he made while rifling the contents of the cupboard, she'd really gotten under his skin.

She almost smiled at the evidence of her tiny victory, but her stomach knotted, sensual hunger licking every erogenous zone, making her fidget as she waited.

Never had she been alone with him like this. She'd also never had his undivided attention.

A slow, simmering thrill of anticipation kept her body taut, her nipples beading against the thickly padded bra. Heat pulsed from deep inside her belly, beginning a slow, heavy thrum that had her tightening her thighs to ease the sweet ache.

Nerves dried her mouth and thickened her tongue. For a cowgirl who always had a smart-ass one-liner ready to aim at anyone who made her feel less than sure of herself, her mind was drawing a complete blank.

Which left her off balance. Uncertain how to proceed.

With any other man, she wouldn't have been strung this tight. But this was Brand.

Although she'd known her share of handsome men, Brand had always been the one who set the standard. At times, especially when another man let her down, she wondered if she hadn't built Brand up in her imagination until he'd reached mythic, unrealistic proportions.

He'd become the hero of all her girlish fantasies, bigger than life, the cowboy riding in to save the day.

When just a glimpse of his tall, muscular frame or the echo of his deep, rumbling voice could make her teeth grind against her aching need, she knew she had a problem.

For a long time now, she'd thought maybe she could whittle him down to "human" if they could spend a little one-on-one time together. Just to get him out of her system once and for all.

Today's little disaster had provided her the unexpected means of achieving a long-held dream. If she played this right, she might finally have a chance of breaking past Brand's steely code of honor that put "Mac's kid sister" strictly off limits.

Excitement shivered through her body. Satisfaction at how well things were progressing bolstered her confidence. She might already have succeeded in knocking a good-sized dent in his intentions if the flavor and the frequency of the muttered curses coming from the pantry were any indication.

Lyssa had never used feminine wiles to get her way with men before, preferring a more direct tack. Today she was quickly discovering she possessed a whole bag of naughty tricks.

When he'd halted the horse next to the porch, he'd dismounted and waited impatiently for her to follow. Instead she'd bitten her lip and given him a worried, helpless look, holding a hand over her chest as though afraid to pull the wound at the top of her breast.

He'd paused, his gaze darkening with suspicion, but he'd reached up, his fingers warming every inch of flesh he gripped to help her down.

Not quite finished, she'd swayed for a moment, not having to exaggerate her breathlessness as his large hands firmed around her sides to hold her steady.

They'd stood so close her chest touched his, and her fingers dug deep into his bare shoulders.

Brand's nostrils flared, and his gaze narrowed on her face, dropping to her lips when she licked them deliberately.

His mouth opened slightly. His chest lifted on an indrawn breath. A moment later he'd dropped his hands—as if she'd scorched his fingers—and stepped back. "Can you walk?" he gritted out, his glance rising stoically above her shoulder.

"Of course," she replied, turning on her heels to hide a grin. She felt the burn of his hot glare on her backside all the way to the kitchen. Naturally she'd exaggerated the sway of her hips, wagging her ass just enough so he wouldn't know she did it on purpose.

She was really getting the hang of this damsel-in-distress act. Sure, the scrapes she'd suffered burned like fire, but a deeper, slower-building heat settled in her core.

Brand had to be feeling the lick of that same flame singeing his heels, or he wouldn't be taking so long to find that damn first-aid kit. "You get lost in there?" she asked, raising her voice above his bad-tempered rumbling.

"Found it!" he called back, his tone no different than when he'd been cussing.

When he backed out of the pantry and turned, his face appeared etched in stone, lips drawn into a thin line. "You're gonna have to lose the shirt, Lyssa," Brand growled as he approached, a plastic box gripped tightly in one hand.

Lyssa sucked in a sharp breath, a little shocked at how

bluntly he'd said it and a whole lot excited by the tension flexing the sides of his square jaw.

"Sure." She reached for the buttons, looking down to hide the delight that had to be dancing in her eyes.

He bit out a soft curse and stomped toward the mudroom. He was back a moment later with a towel crumpled in his hands. "Use this to cover up," he said, holding it out to her.

Lyssa glanced up, her fingers pausing on the third button down. She wouldn't have minded him watching her strip, but then she remembered the bra. "You gonna turn around?" she asked, snatching the towel from him.

"Yeah, sure," he mumbled and turned his back.

A smile tugged her lips at how rattled he looked. His shoulders were rigid, his hands balled into fists.

Her smile slipped when she shrugged out of her shirt and pulled at the dried blood sticking the shirt to her shoulder. She stifled a gasp, yanked to free the material, and felt a fresh trickle of blood run down her back.

She quickly eased off the bra, hid it beneath her shirt and pushed both across the kitchen table. Then she picked up the towel and held it against her chest. After a deep, steadying breath, she whispered, "I'm ready."

"I'm not," he muttered, slowly turning but keeping his gaze averted.

"Too bad," she drawled. "You could have just dumped me on my own porch and let one of the hands clean me up."

"Don't think I'm not regretting it."

"What's got you so bothered, Brand?" she asked innocently.

He snorted and, still clutching the kit, knelt at her side. His fingers lifted a lock of red hair. For just a second, his thumb brushed the end of the lock back and forth, as though he was distracted by its texture, and then he slid the hair over the back of her opposite shoulder, his hand brushing the surface of her hot skin.

She barely suppressed a delighted shiver at his touch.

"That's a nasty gash," he said softly. "Your shots up to date?"

"Afraid I'll bite and give you something?" she quipped, amazed she could speak past the lump lodged at the back of her throat.

A daub with an alcohol-soaked cotton ball forced air hissing between her teeth.

"Sorry about that," he said, his tone laconic. "Have to disinfect."

"You don't sound sorry at all."

"True. It's your own damn fault you're in this predicament."

She aimed a hot glare his way, but his gaze was on her shoulder, his eyebrows drawn into a fierce frown as he gently patted the puncture.

"That hurts," she huffed.

"I know. Has to burn like fire." He leaned close, his glance rising to meet hers as she looked over her shoulder to see what he'd do next.

His lips slowly puckered, and he blew a short, cooling gust over the wound, drying the alcohol. "That better?" he asked slowly, his expression saying nothing of what he really thought.

She nodded quickly, her nipples prickling against the soft terry cloth.

Before she could thank him, he'd pressed a bandage over the puncture.

"The bleeding stopped. I don't think you'll need stitches. Can you handle the other?"

The hopeful note in his voice made her lips twitch. Time to cut the cowards from the rest of the herd.

With one hand holding the front of the towel against her chest, she used the other to hold her hair securely to the side. Lyssa wet her lips and dropped her voice. "Seems my hands are full at the moment."

His gaze fell to her mouth.

Success. She pouted.

His lips firmed, and his brown eyes narrowed. "This will take only a minute. Then I'm bundlin' you into the truck and takin' you home."

She wondered if he realized he'd repeated himself, making it seem like he was the one needing the reminder. He paused so long she knew he sought another option.

Time for a challenge. She lifted her chin. "Well? You gonna do it?" she taunted him. "Or do you want me to wait for Danny? We always got along real good."

Brand shook his head, a small, tight smile curving his lips. "Never know when to quit, do you?"

"Not when it comes to you."

Their gazes locked for a long, charged moment. Then, without bothering to reply, he reached for another cotton ball.

Lyssa couldn't take her gaze off his hands as he tipped the alcohol to soak the fluffy cotton and then lifted it close to her chest.

She straightened in her chair, her body tensing as he slid it over the angry scratch beaded with dried blood. Her lips pursed as she drew in a deep breath at the hot sting.

He swabbed it carefully and then tossed away the cotton and leaned close. His lips were only an inch from the top of her breast.

Lyssa squinted at the ceiling, knowing there was no way in hell he'd think this was an accident. But she couldn't help herself. Didn't even attempt to fight the wicked urge.

She opened the fingers gripping the top of the towel and let it fall—just far enough for one pink nipple to peek above the white terry cloth.

Brand froze. "You dropped something," he said slowly.

"Seems I did," she whispered.

His breath caught . . . and then gusted again, this time aimed at the nipple quickly beading into a ripening point.

Her breasts were small; she knew it. Just as well he'd see for himself what she had to offer. As her breaths grew shallow, her chest quivered.

Afraid to do anything that would break the spell holding his lips hovering just above her nipple, she waited.

He stopped blowing, and his breath hitched. A sound rumbled from deep inside his chest—a strangled groan—and then his head dipped lower. His mouth opened.

The seconds stretched unbearably as she watched him struggle with himself, his shoulders tightening, his hands lifting to grip the edges of her seat as though he didn't trust himself not to grab her.

At last his mouth closed around her straining nipple, his lips scooping up the tip. Another groan tore from his throat as his eyes squeezed shut. He clamped his lips around the nipple and tugged.

A glorious sensation flooded Lyssa—the rhythmic pull of his mouth had its answer in the shallow undulations of her hips sliding on the smooth chair.

Lyssa slowly lifted her hands, not wanting to spook him, and gently cupped the back of his head, spearing her fingers through his short hair. Her thighs eased open around his naked sides as he bent closer and slowly mouthed her breast.

Her head fell back while heat pooled between her legs, her legs clasping and relaxing in time with the soft, short caresses of his lips and tongue.

A shiver worked its way up his body, vibrating against her inner thighs.

Moisture seeped from deep inside her. Her pussy began to pulse, readying her body for invasion.

His tongue stroked the tip of her nipple, swirling on it, and then his teeth bit gently around it.

Lyssa couldn't hold back a moment longer and moaned softly, tightening her grip on his scalp.

Suddenly Brand stiffened. His mouth opened and released her breast. His head sagged, his forehead resting for a moment on her shoulder. Jagged breaths shuddered through his torso. "I'm sorry. That should never have happened."

Lyssa bit back a howl of protest and instead gritted out, "Well, it did. And I'm not sorry." Her hands loosened their grip on his short hair and slipped down to rest atop his shoulders.

His head lifted but remained bowed. "But I am. You're Mac's sister."

Frustrated that he'd deny them both, she snapped, "I'm not a little girl. I'm not some damn virgin."

"But you're not the kind of woman I fuck." At last his gaze met hers, self-recrimination tightening his lips.

"What kind is that?" she asked in an anguished whisper.

His eyes darkened. "A woman who doesn't expect more than a good time."

The bitter heat in his voice struck her, but she hid the wince. Instead she lifted her chin, giving him a steady look. "I don't expect forever, Brand."

"You should." He abruptly hauled himself up to his feet, turned his back, and strode toward the door. "Get your shirt on," he said over his shoulder. "I'm takin' you home."

Lyssa let out a frustrated breath, listening to his boots stomp through the house. She gazed down at herself—at the angry scratch at the top of her breast. At the nipple he'd teased into an exquisitely sensitive point.

Mac had told her a long time ago he never expected Brand to marry. After Brand's mother had run off with a younger man and left Brand's father devastated, Brand had kept his liaisons strictly sexual.

Lyssa thought she might want to try some of that. If Brand could make her wet with just a look—could make her nearly come with just his mouth on her breast—*damn*, what might happen if he let himself go?

Seemed he only noticed her when she caused trouble. So trouble was what she'd stir up.

She dressed slowly, her shoulder stiff, a dull ache pounding behind her eyes. Shuffling to the pickup, she met his gaze above the steering wheel. Something told her another helpless act would only make him mad.

So she climbed inside, slammed the door with a grimace, and buckled up.

Without a word, he started the engine and gunned the gas, making the pickup jerk forward. They spoke at the same time.

"Look—"

"Lyssa—"

"You go ahead," she said, her voice soft.

"What I did . . ." he said, staring at the road ahead. "I apologize."

"You already said that. Two words I didn't want to hear then, so don't bother repeating them now."

His fingers tightened on the steering wheel. "It was a mistake. A natural male reaction, but it won't happen again. So don't get any ideas."

Her anger began a slow boil. He dismissed her feelings completely as if his opinion on the matter was the only one that counted.

"Don't worry about it, Brand," she said, keeping her tone casual. "I just have an itch to scratch. I'll find someone else to sink my claws into."

After a long pause, his roughened voice ground out, "You already have someone in mind?"

Because he expected all women to act like whores, she tossed back her hair, pushing aside any doubts about the crudeness of what she suggested. "I'm heading into Honkytonk tomorrow night. I figure the first unattached man who asks will do just fine."

Brand's hands tightened on the steering wheel. "You think that's safe? Or smart?"

She leveled her gaze on his rigid profile. "Safe and smart would have been me fucking you. But because you aren't attracted, I guess I'll just take my chances."

"Damnit, Lyssa. I never said I wasn't attracted—"

"But you aren't interested."

"I'm not the man for you, Lyssa. But that doesn't mean you should be chasin' after any bastard wearin' a hard-on."

Lyssa's anger slowly began to dissipate. Brand was never anything but polite when talking to her. The thought of her trolling for another man must have bothered him a helluva lot. "Well, it's a good thing you're not wearin' one, isn't it? 'Cause I'm gonna do a whole lot more than chase."

The drive down the caliche-paved ranch road was finished in silence. From the corner of her eye, she watched his eyes narrow to fierce slits and his jaws grind tight.

She knew he fought an internal battle, but what could he say and not look like a hypocrite? His mouth had suckled her nipple as if he were a desperate man.

He'd been gentle and restrained, but every muscle in his shoulders and chest had flexed and bulged as he'd gripped her chair—like he had to hold on to something or risk losing it completely. With her.

No way in hell would Brand let her make good on her threat. Not with the quiet rage that radiated throughout his body.

He'd tell himself he had to stop her because of his promise to her brother, but Lyssa knew better. She might spend more time with her horse than any man, but she was still a woman—and she knew when a man was interested.

Brand might know she was his for the taking, but he didn't know how deep her feelings really went. Maybe she could convince him she really was only after the sex. That was a concept he could relate to.

Lyssa didn't want any old cowboy. If she let him know, the battle would be over before she'd even begun to wage her war for his brand of loving.

3

Brand strode stiffly through the roadhouse bar, doing his best to ignore the brash blare of music from the jukebox and the dancers circling the dark floor. If Lyssa held to her vow, this is where she'd be.

Instead he edged close to his brother, who sat on a bar stool, a beer in one hand while he fingered the edge of a small piece of paper with the other hand. The paper was likely something he'd pulled from the cluttered bulletin board behind the bar.

Leaning on the counter, Brand released a deep sigh. "What is it this time? A ranch in Wyoming need a hand?"

Danny glanced up and gave him a crooked smile. "No, this one's closer to home. A woman with horses."

"Are you talking about Wasp Creek Ranch a couple of counties over? I heard they were looking for wranglers."

Danny nodded and glanced back at the paper, his broad shoulders already tightening.

And because Brand had so much on his mind—the usual

frustrations with running his own ranch, keeping an eye on Lyssa, and trying to rein in the wildness inside his younger brother—he just shook his head.

Could his life get any more complicated? Danny had never been satisfied with his inheritance, had always been eager to shake off the dust of the ranch and roam. Add Lyssa to the equation, and Brand had all the ingredients for a truly explosive cocktail. She wasn't just one more complication—she was its molten center.

Sure, he had a ranch to run with a brother who was itching to strike out on his own—and loneliness that crept like a ghost through his empty house, threatening to rise up and smother him at times—but he'd made a promise to his father to look after his brother. Similar to the one he'd made to Mac. The McDonoughs had been the only family he and Danny had known since their own family had cracked apart. Brand would never let his best friend down.

But what was he to do with Lyssa? She possessed the stubbornness and temper to go along with her long, red hair. And for some unknown reason, she'd gotten it into her mind she wanted him.

Didn't she know he wasn't good enough for someone like her?

If he didn't know how to hold a family together any better than his father had known, how could he satisfy one hard-headed woman?

Brand took a deep breath. Maybe Danny needed to find his own way. "Do what you have to," he said, feeling old and tired. "Your half of the ranch will still be here when you come back."

Danny's head lifted. His eyes widened. "You mean it?"

"I wouldn't have said it if I didn't. At least the place isn't too far away."

"If you need anything . . ."

Brand nodded, forcing a tight smile. "It's not like you to fish in the same pond twice. Didn't you work with the Dermotts' horses when you were in high school?"

"Can't believe you remembered that," Danny muttered, ducking his head.

Something about his evasiveness made Brand suspicious. "Ms. Dermott made quite an impression," he said carefully. "You talked about her for weeks after you came home."

Danny cleared his throat. "She's mighty pretty."

"And a widow now. . . ." The situation was becoming clearer.

His brother's cheeks reddened, and he ducked his head. "I'm too young for her."

Brand's eyebrows rose. So that was it. "How soon were you planning to leave?"

"I haven't applied for the job yet."

"Think there's a chance she won't hire you?"

Danny shrugged and looked away, color rising higher in his cheeks. "I guess not. I'm good with horses."

Brand knew no one in their right mind would turn down Danny—especially if they were already familiar with his talent with horses. Unless the widow had another reason. . . .

Danny swiveled on his stool and rested his elbows on the bar behind him. "So, big brother, when are you going to do something about her?" he asked, jerking his chin toward the dance floor.

Brand didn't remark on the abrupt change of topic. He gritted his teeth, keeping his back to the room but cutting his brother a sideways glance. "About who?"

Danny snorted. His brown eyes danced with mischief. "I know you didn't come here to see me. So don't even try to pretend you aren't here to put a halt to her foolishness. She's dancin' with Cody Westhofen, for fuck's sake!"

"She been here long?" Brand asked quietly.

"Long enough to have most of the men in this room ready to break heads to get at her."

Brand stilled, his shoulders going rigid. "Why would you think I'm gonna do anything about it?"

"Because Lyssa McDonough's the only woman who gets under your skin. You and I both know damn well it's just been a matter of time." Danny gave him a rueful grin. "I hate to be the one to break it to you, bro, but Lyssa's all grown up."

Brand gripped the edge of the counter, wanting to turn and find her on the dance floor but knowing he shouldn't give Danny the satisfaction of being right. He'd never hear the end of it.

"Danny, you and Lyssa are the same age. Did you ever . . . ?"

The thought of his younger brother anywhere near the spitfire knotted his belly.

Danny raised one dark brow, a grin splitting his face. "We went out a time or two in high school, but I never had her. She's particular." He shook his head. "Although what the hell she's doing with Cody . . ."

Brand wished Danny would quit mentioning the bastard's name. *Goddamn,* Cody Westhofen. Of all the men for her to choose . . .

A mug slid down the counter, halting just in front of Brand. He glanced up to find Honkytonk's owner, Tara Toomey, smiling from the opposite end of the bar.

"Need a little Dutch courage?" she asked, raising her voice to be heard above the riff of guitar music as a new song came up.

Brand aimed a blistering glare her way, but Tara only threw back her curly, blond hair and laughed. He raised the glass, sucked the foamy head off the top, and downed a good half of the beer in a single gulp. However, the brew did nothing to cool the heat of his quickly spiking temper.

Slowly he turned to face the dance floor, his gaze panning the crowd.

Although Honkytonk's lone bar was as crowded as usual for a Friday night, with cowboys kicking off a week's dust after riding herd and tourists in cowboy gear looking to snap pictures with the real thing, Brand had no trouble at all finding her.

Wearing a figure-hugging, black tank top tucked into a tight pair of faded blue jeans, Lyssa was impossible to miss.

Her red hair gleamed like a beacon under the stage's muted light as she danced with Cody Westhofen.

If that's what you called what they were doing.

Brand's jaws clamped shut at the sexy spectacle she made of herself, her back snuggled up against Cody's front, his fingers jammed into her front pockets as they danced so close there was no mistaking the message she delivered.

If Brand didn't do something quick, Lyssa would make good on her promise to scratch an itch with the baddest boy in Honkytonk.

"You plannin' to drink the rest of that beer or chew the glass?"

Brand's head swiveled to catch a wry grin from Tara. Because he was beyond polite conversation, he raised his glass and poured it down his throat.

The corners of Tara's blue eyes wrinkled as her smile widened. "Guess I would have lost that bet."

Brand snorted and slammed down the glass on the wooden counter.

"Well, you gonna do something about it?" Danny repeated, a challenge in his glance.

"Mind your own damn business."

"He's minding mine," Tara quipped. "I'm just hopin' to direct the damages out of doors."

"I'm not gonna fight him."

"No? Looks like he's gettin' a little friendlier than your girl wants."

Even though Brand had sworn he wouldn't give them the satisfaction, he couldn't resist. He darted a glance back toward the dance floor. "She's not my gi—" Brand's fists curled. Every muscle in his body knotted.

Cody had turned Lyssa and cupped her sweet little ass. Lyssa appeared to be laughing, but her hands tugged his upward as she squirmed inside his embrace.

Brand pushed away from the bar and strode straight through the crowd, stopping directly behind Lyssa. He aimed a deadly glare at Cody, whose gaze lifted and then narrowed into irritated slits when he saw Brand.

"Don't even try to cut in, Tynan," Cody grated.

Brand shook his head and braced both feet apart. "I believe this is my dance."

Lyssa leaned as far away as Cody's roaming hands would allow and looked over her shoulder. "Fancy finding you here, cowboy."

Brand didn't miss the breathless quality of her voice. Her eyes were wild, and she was more worried than she let on.

Good. When he was done with her . . .

"It's our party, Tynan. Why don't you just move along?"

Cody's words sounded a little slurred. His cheeks were flushed and his eyes a little glazed.

Brand had a clearheaded advantage over the other man, but he didn't care. Not so long as Cody's hands still slipped dangerously low. But he didn't want Lyssa in range when things went sour.

"Lyssa?" he said, barely keeping his tone low and even but giving her an unmistakable choice.

She let go of Cody's hands and pushed against Cody's chest.

"It's all right. Just a dance. Why don't you go get us a couple drinks?"

Cody's expression darkened when he looked down at Lyssa. "Promise not to disappear?"

"Where am I gonna go, Cody?" She glanced up at him from beneath her dark eyelashes. "It's just a dance."

Cody slowly unwound his arms from her body and stepped away, giving her a quick, hot once-over that had Brand's body boiling before the other man carried himself off to the bar without even a nod toward Brand.

Lyssa faced him and lifted her small, round chin. "You said you wanted to dance."

Brand stared for a moment, caught between wanting to shake her and needing to feel her body under his. He forced himself to take a deep breath, tamping down the desire tightening his muscles to steel.

Something in his face must have betrayed his thoughts. Her expression changed, a subtle shift from angry defiance to a wary alarm that widened her eyes and had her backing up a step.

His hands snaked out, gripping her waist. Then he pulled her hard against him. The warmth of her skin burned him through their clothing. "How long's he been with you tonight?" he ground out.

"I came with him," she responded breathlessly. With her arms trapped against his chest, she shoved once, squirming for a moment before giving him a disgruntled frown. "He called me and asked me out."

Brand watched her, noting the flush burning her cheeks and the way her full lips pouted. Gathering her closer, he said softly, "Before or after I dropped you at your place?"

Lyssa stiffened in his arms, her lips pressing into a mutinous line. "That's none of your business."

The music changed to a slower tune, and the overhead lights dimmed.

Resignation filled him, and he slid his hands around her back, gliding straight toward the lush curve of her ass. He thrust his knee between her thighs and pulled her belly flush against the ridge hardening beneath his fly, ignoring her gasp.

He bent closer, lifting his thigh to rub against her pussy. "Before or after I dropped you at your place, Lyss?" he repeated, keeping his tone even.

"After," she breathed. Her body jerked as he rubbed higher, and her hips undulated, beginning to ride his thigh.

Leaning down, he whispered against her ear. "Are you trying to teach me a lesson, sweetheart?"

Lyssa's shortened breaths feathered across his cheek. "Doesn't have a thing to do with you."

"*Liar.*"

"You said you weren't interested. He is."

"He's only interested in getting inside those tight jeans."

She tossed back her hair and glared straight into his eyes. "And that's a bad thing?" she asked, her voice strengthening. "I told you I have an itch."

Brand narrowed his gaze. "I'm takin' you home."

Her eyes flashed green fire. "*You* are not my brother."

"Someone needs to keep a closer eye on you."

Her chin lifted impossibly higher. "I'm old enough to do whatever I please with Cody," she said, acid in her tone. "Man's got himself quite a reputation."

"Do you want to be just another notch on his bedpost?"

One dark brow arched. "Why not? He seems to know his way around a woman's body."

His hands tightened on her bottom, biting into the soft flesh. "You're not gonna back down, are you?"

"No . . . I'm not." Her eyelashes lowered and then swept up to reveal a steady, green gaze. "Are you?"

Despite her bravado, Brand could feel the way she melted all over him, her thighs clutching his, her breasts and belly softening, her body blending with his movements.

The thought that she might have been just as eager with Cody had his blood buzzing. "Just what do you want, Lyssa?"

Her cheeks darkened, flushing a deep rose he could see even in the dim light. Her gaze slid away.

Hell if he'd let her ignore him. Brand reached up and gripped her hair, tugging firmly to tilt back her head. "Tell me," he said, his lips hovering above hers.

"You, damnit," she said softly. "I want you."

Brand relaxed as satisfaction filled him. He eased his grip. "What about you and Cody?"

She wet her lips with a quick, nervous swipe of her tongue. "He's just a substitute. You know that."

Taking his other hand from her rounded backside, he cupped her chin, lifting her gaze to lock with his. "Did you let him touch you? Before you got here?"

Her lips parted, and her eyes instantly filled.

Damn. Cold, thickening anger chilled his blood. "Did you let him touch you, Lyss?"

She shrugged, trying to smile, but the corners of her lips drew down. "Not much."

"Define 'not much,' " he bit out.

She swallowed hard. "What's it to you?"

"I'm not asking. You tell me."

Her eyes slid away again. "We kissed in his truck." She paused and cleared her throat. "He felt me up a bit."

Brand's jaw ground tight. "Your breasts?"

She nodded sharply.

"More?" Another quick nod, and he leaned over her, digging his fingers deep into her hair.

Her breath caught. "I was angry . . . with you."

"Lyssa . . ." he said, his voice rising in warning.

"He . . . um, slid his hand inside my pants," she said in a rush, "but I stopped him."

A quiver of rage seethed through him. "Did he touch your pussy?"

Lyssa closed her eyes and leaned her head against his shoulder. "No. I swear I stopped him."

Brand sucked in a deep, cleansing breath, trying to clear away his anger, and then tilted back her head. "Don't ever lie to me, Lyssa."

Her green eyes opened, glittering from unshed tears. "I wouldn't."

"I'm takin' you home now."

She nodded, her gaze clinging to his almost as tightly as her hands clamped his stiff shoulders.

He liked that look. Wanted it there every time he commanded something of her. Not that he didn't like a little defiance, too.

Brand let go of the sinking sensation that filled him every time he thought about what it would be like to command her in bed.

Mac wouldn't like it. Might even want to kick his ass.

Brand might let him. But he couldn't let Lyssa walk into another man's arms. "Get your purse."

He let her go, giving her a gentle shove toward the bar, noting how she avoided the far end where Cody stood staring after her.

Cody's glance swung back toward Brand and narrowed. He pushed away from the counter.

"Damn! Guess there's gonna be a fight after all," Brand muttered.

Lyssa walked like an automaton toward the bar and stepped behind it, bending low to reach under the ledge into the cubbyhole in which she'd stashed her purse. She didn't dare think beyond the moment, or she'd start shaking so hard she'd never get out the door.

"Better hurry up," Tara murmured just above her. "You're gonna miss the fireworks."

"What?" Lyssa came up sharply, banging her head on the counter. "Ow." When she straightened, she turned her gaze toward the floor to find it quickly clearing. Brand and Cody circled each other, their glances already locked in quiet combat.

"Brand sure didn't like seeing you with Cody," Tara drawled.

"Brand's not gonna fight him. Not over me." She rubbed the sore spot.

Tara snorted. "You didn't see him before he decided to cut in."

"Oh?" She shot Tara a veiled glance. "Did he say something to you?"

"Hardly spoke a word." Tara waggled her eyebrows. "Mostly growled."

Lyssa pretended indifference, though she was secretly thrilled. "He just likes playing big brother. Probably thought Mac would have my ass for even talking to Cody."

"The man does have a wicked reputation." Tara's gaze swung back, and she lifted one brow. "That why you asked him out?"

Lyssa scowled. "How'd you know I asked him?"

"If I was trying to get Brand mad enough to declare himself, that's exactly who I'd have chosen. He's good-lookin'. Women come easy to him. . . ."

"He's a damn good cowboy."

"Never saw a harder worker—whether it was working cattle or a horny woman."

"Tara!"

"Don't even try to tell me you didn't consider it."

Heat seared Lyssa's cheeks. "I've been waiting on that Tynan man forever. Would you blame me?"

Wicked amusement gleamed in Tara's blue eyes. "Not a bit."

They shared a smile and glanced back at the dance floor where the two men were slowly rolling up their sleeves.

"Aren't you gonna try to stop them?" Lyssa asked softly.

"Why? They can't do any damage there. 'Sides, it's good for business. The tourists love it."

Lyssa didn't. She also didn't miss the many curious and judging looks that came her way. "Think either of them will even notice if I sneak out of here?"

Tara gripped her by the shoulders and turned her to face the floor. "Think I'm gonna let you slink out of here when one of those handsome men remembers who started this?"

"Tell me you don't still have a soft spot for Cody."

Tara wrinkled her nose. "The man needs to be taken down a peg or two before he looks a little lower down the ladder."

Lyssa drew back. Tara might be in her mid-forties, but she was still an attractive woman. "You think you're not good enough?"

The other woman's smile seemed a little too tight to be real. "I'm a little older than him."

"Not by much."

"He can have anyone he wants."

Lyssa shook her head. "Not me."

"Could have fooled me, girlfriend."

"I just wanted to fool Brand." Lyssa grabbed Tara's hand and squeezed it. "I'm sorry."

"Don't be. Cody only comes around when he's . . . in between."

Lyssa's eyes widened. "Oh!"

"Don't look so surprised. I have almost everything I ever wanted." She let out a deep sigh. "And I'm patient."

"I'm not," Lyssa said, wincing as Cody's fist connected with the side of Brand's square jaw.

"Is your lack of patience what tonight's all about?"

"Maybe." Lyssa couldn't keep her mind on the conversation. Her stomach tensed as Brand's fist smashed into Cody's rock-hard abdomen.

Tara winced. "That had to hurt."

"Hurt who?"

"See your point."

Cody swung again at Brand's face, but Brand ducked beneath the blow and landed two quick punches against Cody's ribs.

Cody backed up, and his heel caught the edge of the parquet dance floor. His arms windmilled for a moment, and then he crashed to the floor.

A loud chorus of disappointed moans rose from the crowd.

Lyssa had had enough. She tucked her purse under her arm and moved around the bar to sidle up next to Brand. "About that ride . . ." she said, tugging on his raised arm.

Brand's head turned to her. He gave Cody one more glare and straightened, dropping his arms. He lifted his chin toward the door.

Lyssa ignored the snickers that followed her out of the bar and into the parking lot. She kept her head held high and marched stiffly toward Brand's big, black Ford.

She avoided his glance when he opened the door for her, and she stepped up into the cab.

Brand walked around the front of the truck, rolling down

his sleeves. When he'd closed the buttons at the cuffs, he raised his gaze to meet hers through the glass.

An expression transformed his features—something so primal and deeply masculine her whole body clenched.

Maybe tonight's little drama had been overkill, but she couldn't regret a moment. Brand had never looked at her like that before.

Like he'd won the right to do whatever he wanted with her.

When he climbed into the cab, the air crackled with tension. He twisted the key, set the truck in gear, and hit the gas. The diesel engine growled like a cougar, filling the silence between them.

Several minutes later, Brand drew a deep, tense breath. "Did you like it when he touched you?"

She shot him a glance, wondering how she should answer. Whether she had the courage to ratchet his anger higher. She turned back to stare through the windshield, afraid to push him harder. Still, he wasn't past control.

Clouds obscured the moon and stars, blanketing the wide sky. The twin beams cut a narrow path through the murky darkness.

"Lyss! Did you like it?"

Lyssa cleared her throat and shrugged. "I guess."

Brand swung the wheel sharply to the right and hit the brakes, sending a spray of gravel to rattle against the mud flaps.

So abrupt was his action, she didn't have time to think when he slammed open his door and stomped around the truck. Her door jerked open, and steely fingers wrapped around her wrist, yanking her from the truck, straight into his arms.

"*You guess?*"

4

Brand's expression was so dark, so intense, all Lyssa could do was shiver. Over the years of their long acquaintance, she'd seen him angry more than a few times.

Sure, his temper blew hot. Was aimed always at the result, never the person. Completely fair. But it faded quickly once he'd dealt with whomever or whatever caused him to erupt.

This was different. Intriguing. *And, oh, so arousing.* This time his anger built like rainfall gathering in arroyos that spilled into a dry creek until its crumbling banks overflowed.

Her mouth dropped open. She'd wanted to make him lose control—but had she pushed him too far? She quickly clamped her lips shut.

Shocked by his reaction, she didn't know how to respond. Although she'd goaded him into this, she trembled beneath his hot glare and remained silent, deciding to err, for once, on the side of caution.

Brand's hot breaths gusted against her face. His lips thinned;

his nostrils flared. A wildness entered his expression, melting her insides like hot wax.

His heated glare raked her face and then dropped to her lips.

Desire liquefied her core, curling inside her belly, sending blood rushing south to pulse between her legs. Overcome, her lips parted, and a thin moan slipped between them.

Brand bit back a soft curse and then dove. His mouth slammed into hers before she could suck in a breath to fill her empty lungs.

The kiss—a brutal, biting mashing of teeth and lips—didn't gentle, didn't slow.

Brand backed her against the side of the truck, pressing his body against hers, grinding his thickening erection into her abdomen. His hands slammed against the metal on either side of her shoulders, and he leaned closer.

Lyssa took the kiss, opening her mouth to breathe, and then groaned when his tongue pushed inside and he continued to ravage her mouth.

Every part of him was hard—shuddering, driving into her.

Her body reacted instantly, flooding her pussy with melting heat, sending a quivering excitement throughout her wilting, surrendering body.

The tension in his shoulders and rock-hard abs radiated rage, but his thick, guttural groans betrayed something else.

Frustration? Disappointment? Had she hurt him?

Her legs wobbled, and she felt herself sliding down.

Afraid that maybe she'd blown it, she began to sob, clutching at his arms to hold herself upright.

She'd been wrong. Selfish. Childish even. But, dear God, she'd needed to break him. She hadn't realized that only a slender thread had held his temper and his desire in check. Once he cooled off, would he push her away? Become disgusted with his reaction? Or, worse, with her?

Brand jerked back his head, breaking the kiss, and eased away from her body. His hands, however, remained on the truck, bracketing her shoulders. His sharp gaze glittered in the darkness.

Lyssa's swollen lips trembled along with her legs, and she relaxed against the truck, letting the moment stretch between them as she dragged in deep, harsh breaths.

Despite her trepidation, a languorous heat filled her. Her head fell back against metal, and her breasts lifted with her jagged gasps, jutting against the thin material of the insubstantial bra she'd chosen tonight.

Brand's head dipped. Expecting another kiss, she nearly slid to the ground when his nose and lips glided along the neckline of her tank top, his tongue sweeping out to lick at the sweat gathering between her breasts.

Then his mouth grazed over the fabric, giving her shielded bites that had her straining upward until, at last, his lips closed around a beaded nipple.

Warmth seeped through the fabric. His teeth nipped at a tightening bud. Lyssa reached up and thrust her fingers though his thick hair, trying to press her breast deeper into his mouth.

A low growl ripped through him, and he reached up and dragged her hands from his hair, his fingers biting into her wrists. Then he quickly turned her, forcing her against the truck.

His head bent close; his breath feathered her cheek. "Did you like it when he touched you?" he rasped.

Lyssa was so aroused now she couldn't gather the remnants of her pride, couldn't summon her wits to find the answer she needed to disarm him. "N—noooo!" she moaned brokenly, a soft sob vibrating through her body.

His hands slipped between her and the truck, sliding over her breasts, cupping them, squeezing and then gliding lower.

Another sob shook her, and she struggled against his unhurried touch as he smoothed down the outside of her hips and then up again.

Dragging the hem of her shirt out of her pants, he shoved the fabric upward, bunching it beneath her arms.

When his palms flowed around her belly and upward to slip beneath her bra, she didn't resist as he pushed it up, eager for his spreading fingers to cup her naked breasts.

The rasp of his calloused palms on her engorged nipples was electric. She cried out, stiffening, pushing her breasts deeper into his palms.

"God, Lyssa. You're driving me out of my mind," he groaned, clasping her breasts hard.

Suddenly his hands dropped to her hips; he leaned back and jerked her against him. Her head fell against his shoulder, and she grabbed the sides of his thighs to steady herself.

Brand didn't give her a moment to regroup. He flung open her belt, flicked open the button at the top of her jeans, and tugged down her zipper. Then his hand thrust into the opening, his fingers sliding between her legs, straight into her slick folds.

Her knees trembled at his invasion, and her hands plucked at his jeans. The scrape of his fingers as they entered her triggered a gush of liquid. She cried out, and her knees began to crumple.

"This what you wanted?" he asked hoarsely, the hand still gripping her hip the only thing holding her upright. "You want someone, *any man,* inside you?"

Lyssa reached behind her, her hands sliding around his neck as she arched her body into his and widened her stance.

His fingers slid deeper inside, thrusting, twisting into her entrance.

"Yesssss . . . any man, Brand," she lied, quickly growing frantic. "God, fuck me. *Please.*"

* * *

Damn her. Why did she have to be so hot, so goddamn wet?

Although aware of this lonely stretch of road and the fact that anyone might come upon them at any time, he couldn't think beyond the liquid heat surrounding his fingers, the curve of her sweet ass as it rubbed against his cock, and her slender body writhing in his arms.

Adrenaline from the fight still seared his mind. His body shuddered as he pressed deeper, twisting his fingers, stroking into her wild, undulating frame. Soft, shuddering sobs broke from her throat while she pulsed her hips, the movement dragging on his fingers and forcing him deeper.

No way in hell would he walk away from her tonight. Her arousal scented the air, sealing his intent. Because Danny was still hugging a beer at the bar, he could take her home.

Ignoring her protests, he withdrew his fingers and pulled up her zipper. When he'd dragged down her shirt, he ground out, "Get in the truck."

He helped her into the cab, his hand cupping her ass to push her up. Then he reached across her and buckled the seatbelt, gave her a quick, hard kiss, and walked around the front of the truck, adjusting himself.

On the drive home, her darting glances and restless movements betrayed her nervousness.

When he pulled into the driveway, he didn't look her way. "Get out and get on back to my bedroom. Take off all your clothes. I'll be there in a minute."

Her breath huffed out. "I beg your pardon?" she asked incredulously.

Brand nailed her with a stare. "You heard me."

She pushed her shoulder against the door and opened it, sliding off the seat, not looking back once as she stomped up the steps and into the house.

He almost smiled at the stiffness of her posture. Lyssa was

plenty mad, but she hadn't hesitated to do as he told her. Perhaps arousal won out. Or maybe she wanted an even playing field, a chance to gather her shattered defenses before battling with him again.

Funny how he'd always thought he'd want to be gentle with her. Now he knew better. He'd tasted her heat, knew firsthand what set her on fire.

After he put the truck in the garage, he took his time walking back to the house, trying to get control of his anger. Seeing her with Cody, the other man's hands shoved deep in her pockets so he could ride her swaying hips, had driven him crazy.

That she'd given Cody liberties with her body only added to the rage simmering inside him. Had Cody cupped her small breasts through her clothing or slipped a hand inside? Did he know the velvety texture of her nipples?

Brand wished he'd broken the other man's fingers instead of only leaving bruises up and down his ribs.

Stepping onto the porch, he noted the lights blazing a trail through his house, flickering on inside the living room and then the hallway.

He opened the screen and slammed the oak door behind him, letting her know he was on his way. A deep, possessive satisfaction filled him as he imagined her stripping away her clothing with trembling hands and slipping between his cool sheets.

The bedroom door stood open. He strode inside, his gaze flicking over the empty bed.

Lyssa stood at the end of it, still dressed. Her hands were curled into fists at her sides.

He lifted an eyebrow, leaned against the door frame, and folded his arms over his chest. "Tell me if I'm wrong, but I thought this was what you wanted."

Her small, white teeth nibbled at her bottom lip and then released it. "I thought we might take it a little slower."

Her voice sounded strained. Brand shook his head. "I want you out of your clothes. Now."

A scowl drew her auburn brows together. "What is it with you? You're always telling me what to do."

Knowing Lyssa's tendency to balk when unsettled, he let her defiance slide. Maybe she was a little scared. Warmth filled his chest, and he settled deeper against the door. "If you don't like it, you can leave," he said, offering her a crooked smile.

"I don't understand you."

"Maybe I just want to see you naked. A man likes to look."

"Wouldn't it be a little more fun if you helped me . . . *get naked?*"

"Sweetheart, if I help, you might be leaving here in rags tomorrow morning."

A glimmer of a smile began to curve her lips. "Are you telling me you don't feel very civilized?"

Not wanting her to get too sure, he straightened from the door and took a step farther into the room. "Your clothes."

The woman—who never lacked for the just the right word or look to make him crazy—shrugged and gave him a glance that swept his face, lingered on his chest, and slid sinuously down his abdomen to rest between his legs. "I'm not always gonna be this agreeable, cowboy, but, fact is, you've got something I want. *Bad.*"

If he wasn't so hard he could have hammered nails with his cock, he might have laughed at her sultry siren talk. "Lyss, you've been after this for years. Gonna blow your chance now because you pissed me off?"

"Tonight," she huffed. "I won't mind you bein' in charge tonight."

"You'll listen to me here, and you'll listen to what I have to say about the way you run your ranch."

She fisted a hand on her hip. "And if I don't?"

He tilted his head, keeping his expression from revealing how much her continued defiance pleased him. Taming Lyssa would provide endless enjoyment.

Blood pumping, he strode toward her.

Her eyes widened, and she cast a quick glance around her, as though she considered running, but quickly met his gaze again, her chin rising.

He halted in front of her, breathing deeply, catching her scent—a rich cinnamon, flavored with her own light musk.

Sweat gleamed across the top of her chest. He remembered the feel of her small, velvet nipples scraping his tongue, and he swallowed a growl.

He'd never brought a woman to his place, but he wasn't going to think about that fact too much. Lyssa belonged here—for as long as it took to get her out of his system, out of his mind.

A thought lingered like a tantalizing tease. Perhaps he'd never tire of her—and maybe he could keep her so mindless with pleasure she'd never want to leave.

But, first, he needed to impress upon her the importance of obedience. "You played a dangerous game with me tonight, baby."

Lyssa tossed back her hair. "You think that was all about you?"

"I told you—never lie to me."

A hard swallow tensed the muscles of her neck. "All right. So playing with Cody *might* have been about revenge."

His teeth clenched. "Don't say his name again."

"Were you jealous?"

"Jealous is too tame a word, Lyss."

"Will it make you mad if I confess I asked him out?"

For some reason the admission made him smile.

Her gaze narrowed. "Is that an I-could-give-a-shit smile, or are you planning a reprisal?"

"How many times do I have to tell you? I want your clothes." He held out his hand.

Her fingers splayed against her flat belly and then slowly curled and pulled at the fabric. She gripped the cotton and slipped it over her head; then she dropped the shirt onto his hand.

Her bra clasped in front, and she started to turn as she unsnapped it.

"Don't turn away. I want to see."

Her lips crimped. Her chest rose as she took a deep breath; Then she opened the bra and shrugged it off. She caught it just before it fell and draped it across his hand. Only then did she raise her head.

Blood rushed toward his loins, filling his cock.

She was everything he'd remembered. Perfect. An angry, red scratch the only blemish. Barely rounded mounds of creamy flesh, topped with satiny, pale pink cones. He couldn't wait to take another sip, draw on her like a straw until the tips bloomed against his tongue.

"I'm small," she said, her feet shifting restlessly.

"I noticed." His mouth was so dry he didn't trust himself to say more and couldn't worry about her thinking he wasn't pleased. He'd show her soon enough. "The rest," he grated out.

Her cheeks billowed with an exasperated breath, but she sat on the edge of his bed and pulled off her boots, her socks, and then stood to open her belt and jeans, skimming them down her thighs.

The only item of clothing left was a small scrap of black lace arrowing between her hips, dipping between her legs.

"You can keep those on for now," he said when she hooked her thumbs in the thin lace at the sides.

Relief gleamed in her eyes.

He set the clothing she'd given him on a chair beside the door and then faced her. He unbuttoned his cuffs and his shirt, and pulled the tails from his jeans. As he drew the shirt off his shoulders, he watched her gaze skitter over his chest.

Color bloomed brighter on her cheeks, and her breasts rose and fell, her nipples sprouting.

He toed off his boots, stripped away his socks, and unbuckled his belt, drawing it slowly from the loops, but he didn't do more than unsnap the top of his jeans to ease the constriction building in his loins.

Then he walked toward Lyssa, his hands rising to catch the notches of her hips, not stopping until those pretty pink cones scraped his chest.

Lyssa's head fell back, and her eyelids dipped. Her hands tentatively reached up to curve over the tops of his shoulders.

Brand couldn't believe he was finally here, years spent lusting after the fiery-tempered woman nearly at an end.

Staring into her green gaze, he was reminded of Mac. Of his tight face when they'd thrown their arms around each other the moment before he'd boarded the plane. His eyes had bored into Brand as he'd asked him to take care of Lyssa.

Mac sure as hell hadn't meant it like this, but Brand couldn't put her away from him—not now, when her sweet curves quivered beneath his palms.

She wet her lips, her gaze clinging to his face.

He let any last resistance go in a slow exhalation while his hands smoothed up her back, one to cup the back of her head, the other to cradle her body closer to his chest.

When he lowered his head, Lyssa murmured and rose on her toes, meeting his kiss. Her lips rubbed against his and then suctioned softly, her tongue reaching out to stroke his bottom lip until he opened.

Giving her the lead for now, he let her sweep inside, enjoying the press of her body against his as her breaths deepened. He loved the excited little noises escaping her mouth each time she broke the kiss to breathe.

The warmth of her hair, the silky feel of her skin, the flavors exploding on his tongue—all built to a sexy culmination that had him ready to seize the reins. He backed her up to the bed and then pushed her down onto the mattress, grabbing her ankles when she tried to scoot quickly to the center.

Instead he pulled her to the edge, draping her knees over the side, bracketing her thighs with his as he leaned over her to frame her face between his palms and deepen the kiss.

She sighed into his mouth, reaching up to wrap her arms around his shoulders to pull him to her, but he resisted, breaking the kiss to skim the edge of her jaw before gliding south.

He couldn't resist the lure of her pretty little nipples, finding the first one quivering and erect. He stroked the tip, letting the point drag across his tongue before scooping up the entire areola and suckling hard.

Lyssa's back arched, lifting her belly and hips to press against him, so sweetly responsive he fought the urge to rip the silk protecting her sweet cunt to dive right in.

He opened his mouth, rubbed his lips around the tip one more time, and then moved to the other breast.

Her hands threaded through his hair, and she tugged, trying to force him lower.

Only because he hungered for the taste of her arousal did he relent, kissing a path across her trembling belly and backing off the mattress to kneel beside her as he trailed lower.

Soft nudges to her knees met no resistance as she opened eagerly for him, spreading her thighs and shifting her bottom closer to the edge.

Brand moved between her legs, smoothing his hands up and down the outside of her thighs and then skimming his fingertips from her knees upward toward the moist juncture.

He paused just below the scrap of lace.

"Let me take them off," she whispered.

He shook his head. "Not yet." He didn't trust himself. Needed the barrier there to remind him to take it slow and make sure she came along with him for the ride.

"I don't need this, Brand," she said, her voice sounding thin and strained. "I'm there. I swear it."

Brand placed a kiss on one inner thigh and sank back on his haunches. "Sweetheart, this isn't a race. It also isn't about giving you everything you want."

"Are you still playing games?"

"I don't play games. You need to learn who's in charge here."

"This is a mutual thing. I want something. You want something. Just get it the fuck on."

"It happens when I say. Not a second sooner." At her outraged screech, Brand simply smiled.

Then he bent close and pressed his tongue to the wet spot at the center of her silky black panties.

5

Torn between wanting to box him and needing another of those sexy licks, Lyssa moaned and rubbed her calves up and down his sides.

His tongue scraped the silk, prodding through the fabric—delivering a teasing flutter that had her pussy tightening, trying to capture his elusive forays.

When a finger glided along the edge of the elastic at her inner thigh, her breath caught. He slipped under it, tracing the corner where her thigh met her labia and then skimming over the plump outer lip, combing through her short curls before skimming down toward her back entrance—all the while continuing to prod and lick over the silk, wetting her through her underwear.

Uncomfortable with his new direction, she pressed her feet against his thighs and lifted her bottom off the mattress, trying to evade, but he pressed deeper, tracing between her buttocks until he skimmed the little hole.

She gasped, murmured a soft complaint, and dug her toes into his skin.

He pulled his fingers from beneath her panties and skimmed his hands from her ankles up her inner thighs. Then, pressing gently to encourage her to open wider, he leaned into her to suction against her folds, gliding the fabric with his lips and tongue until the slight friction began to weave its magic.

Her knees fell open, her back arched as she pressed her head deeper into the mattress and stared at the white ceiling above her.

Any moment now, his tongue would glance against her clit, and she'd be spiraling toward heaven.

His hands glided higher, finding the elastic of her panties. He leaned back to tug them down her legs, waiting as she lifted her hips so that he could pull them away.

Then she was completely naked, opening for him like a flower, lying pliant, boneless, her breaths shuddering as his hands spread her sex.

His mouth descended again. This time he touched her directly, finding the bud at the top of her folds, his fingers pulling up the hood to expose it to the cooler air and the hot flick of his tongue.

Once, twice, and a gentle convulsion rippled through her vagina. Lyssa pulled at the bedding with her fists and rode the wave while he continued to suckle and stroke her clit.

When the ripples slowed, she relaxed, closing her eyes, breathing deeply, afraid to meet his gaze and let him read too much of what she felt.

She wanted to cry. To howl. To beg him to gather her into his arms and hold her.

Only, that wasn't her. Not the person she thought she was, anyway—and not the good-time girl she wanted to be for him. She knew it would scare the crap out of him.

Instead she gathered her courage and rose up on her elbows to meet his gaze. "Guess you can tell I liked it. A lot."

He didn't answer, just stared, his fingers gliding in the moisture that continued to spill from inside her. Arousal tightened his features, brushing rich, red color across the tops of his sharp cheekbones. His lips were swollen, wet.

She couldn't wait to taste herself when next they kissed.

"I still have that itch," she whispered, trying to pretend she didn't feel vulnerable, her heart and her body ruthlessly exposed.

"Get to the center of the bed," he said.

His tight voice shot a fresh wave of pulsing need straight up her channel. She didn't wait for him to repeat it. Didn't play at defying him. She scooted back as he slowly stood and stripped away his jeans.

When he straightened, her glance snagged on his erection. Engorged, reddened, the skin stretched and satiny.

She licked her lips, hoping he'd let her get acquainted later, because right now she needed to feel the thrust of his large cock stroking deep toward her core.

His lips tightened. "Shit. Just a second." He bent to pick up his jeans, shaking them to dump his wallet to the ground. Then he swiped it up and opened it. His fingers plucked a foil packet from a slot.

Lyssa smiled. She'd forgotten. He almost had as well. Would it have been so bad, wondering whether they'd made a baby? She didn't worry she'd get a thing other than pleasure from him, as cautious as he was around women.

She watched, fascinated, as he ripped the foil with his teeth and then extracted the latex sheath. With a practiced motion, he fit it to the tip of his cock and glided it down.

When it was fully unrolled, his fingers wrapped around his thick shaft, gliding down and then slowly up as his gaze centered on her pussy. Then he crawled onto the mattress, right over her, his broad shoulders blocking out the light from the overhead lamp. His body radiated a heat that warmed her breasts and belly before their skin actually met.

When he settled on top of her, she moaned, opening for him, lifting her knees to hug his hips with her inner thighs.

The tip of his cock nudged between her legs, found her center, and dipped into her moisture.

Just the crown, just enough to give her a hint of pressure, of the fullness she'd experience.

"Don't stop now."

He gritted his teeth, nudging deeper, and settled his knees on the mattress, his hands beside her shoulders. "God, I couldn't even if I tried. There's no going back, Lyss."

"Do it," she whispered.

A long, ragged groan escaped as he thrust, pulsing as he drove inside her, stroking deeper in and out, until at last his cock was fully sheathed.

His head fell to her shoulder, and he rubbed his forehead against it. "You have no idea how goddamn good this feels."

Stretched, filled like she'd never been before, she gasped, "I'm on the receiving end. . . . Believe me . . . I have a clue. *Move? Now?*"

A short, desperate laugh expanded his chest, and then his head came up and slanted, capturing her lips. His hips tightened, flexing. Then he began to move, driving slowly in and out.

Lyssa wasn't having it. Wasn't settling for gentle. She wanted the fireworks, the promise of the sensual violence he'd hinted at when he'd run his truck off the road and forced her to lie about wanting a man, *any man*, banging away at her body.

Breaking the kiss, she raised her legs and hooked them high over his hips and then raked her fingernails down his back until she reached his buttocks and dug in her nails. "I don't want easy," she growled. "Not from you."

"I don't wanna hurt you," he gritted out, continuing his slow glides.

"I'm not gonna break. I might even like a little pain. Fuck me, Brand. *Fuck me hard.*"

"Jesus, Lyss," he said, planting a kiss on her shoulder.

Then his knees crowded closer and he pushed upward, kneeling, forcing her thighs to slip away from his sides. He hooked his arms beneath her knees and dragged her hips off the bed.

His gaze dropped to where their bodies connected, where he slid in and out, slowly.

Lyssa couldn't look away either. Her pussy clasped his cock, her vulva sinking inward, stretching outward with each stroke, leaving moisture glistening along his shaft. Friction built with each thrust, triggering a steady flow of honey and an easing of her tight grasp as he continued to cram his thick cock deep into her body.

Lyssa didn't complain again as his steady, rocking motions fanned the slow-burning tendrils of heat curling around her womb. She closed her eyes, lifted her hands to her breasts, and touched just a fingertip against each, swirling softly on the tips.

Brand's thrust deepened, sharpened. Did he like watching her touch herself? She slitted her eyelids and peered up.

His hard gaze followed the motions of her fingers. He dragged her hips higher and began to plow his cock into her, the gentle rocking growing into steeply pitched waves.

The skin stretched taut against his cheeks darkened. The muscles of his shoulders and arms bunched. The ridges defining his abdomen deepened as he began to slam against the cradle of her sex.

Lyssa's back arched, her mouth opening around an anguished groan. Her fingers clasped her breasts, twisting the nipples just enough to send a dart of electricity zinging toward her core.

She cupped her hips upward to rub her clit against his groin each time he slammed home, gasping as he hammered faster.

Then Brand fell over her, bracing his hands on the mattress, his arms forcing her thighs high and into her chest.

With increased leverage, he hammered harder, thrusting so deep he forced soft, grunting gusts of air from her mouth.

It was too much. Too intense, too hot . . . too desperate.

Her head thrashed on the bed, and she released her breasts, fisting her hands on the coverlet as he slammed her up the bed.

When her orgasm hit, her whole body went rigid, straining against his arms and body, her back bowing, her mouth opening around a scream that stretched like the keening of a wild animal.

"GodohGodohGod! Brand!"

His hips hammered faster, losing rhythm, thrusting wildly, jerking against her as a long, rasping groan tore from his throat and scalding heat stroked into her at the moment of his release.

She wrapped her arms around him as he continued to rock against her. She kissed his ear and cheek and smoothed her hands up and down his back as he shuddered above her.

Tears threatened to spill from her eyes. This moment was almost as good as when she'd exploded in climax. Holding his sweaty body against hers, their ragged breaths shaking their bodies against each other, his cock still embedded deep inside her.

Still connected. Still belonging to each other. If only for a moment. She had to have more of this. More of his loving. More of this sweet, golden aftermath. Whatever it took.

Brand couldn't bear to pull away . . . as he should. Her cunt still rippled up and down his shaft from faint aftershocks. Even through the condom, he could feel the moist, honeyed heat of her grasping him like a stroking fist.

Damn, they were good together. He'd always known instinctively that it would be like this with her.

Which was one reason he'd tried so hard to keep away. He'd been afraid of feeling this way. Complete. Wanting to stay buried deep inside her body until his cock grew thick and he could begin again.

Lyssa stirred beneath him, her body winding around his, hugging him closer with her arms and legs. She murmured and slid her lips along his cheek.

Not able to resist the invitation, he raised his head and angled his mouth to meet hers.

This time, their kiss was as intimate and as deep as the act that bound their bodies together.

Brand fought the countering urges—one to draw away, to break the connection, the other to wrap his arms beneath her body and hold her closer.

When their lips eased apart, she lifted slumberous eyelids. "Do you have more?"

"More?" he asked, a smile beginning to tug his lips. Her face was pink. Her lips blurred from their kiss. She looked so damn sexy, so damn *fucked,* a surge of masculine pride tightened his body.

"Condoms," she said, sounding breathless.

"I'll find more," he said, even as he wondered if he shouldn't be bundling her back into her clothes to take her home. Things were getting sticky fast.

Her lips stretched into a lazy smile. "You don't have to go anywhere right away. I'm a little hungry anyway."

The look that darkened her eyes told him she wasn't talking about a midnight snack. An image of her lush mouth stretching around his cock nearly made him groan. He dove down, sliding his tongue into her mouth to duel with hers. When her lips suctioned his, a growl vibrated through him.

Her hands slipped between their bodies, and she pushed. When their mouths parted, she gave him a steady, challenging look. "Lie back."

"That would mean I'd have to pull out of you, Lyss. Don't think I can."

"I promise I won't let anything stay cold for long." She bit her bottom lip, waiting for him to decide.

Brand reached behind him, gently eased her legs from his hips, and then pushed away from her body, pulling his cock slowly from her juicy cunt.

They both moaned when he finally slipped free.

His gaze locked with hers, and he lay on his back, putting an arm beneath his head and resting a hand on his ribs.

Lyssa stretched beside him and then came up on one elbow to rake his body with a possessive glance. She halted at his cock and reached out, her fingers ringing him beneath the condom, and then slowly pulled up, sliding off the condom.

Brand grabbed it from her, set it on the bedside table, and settled back again.

She knelt next to him, her hands on her thighs as she considered where to start. "Open your legs for me?" she asked, tilting her head. Rich color swept across her tanned cheeks and brightened the pale skin across the tops of her small breasts.

Brand grinned and made a space for her between his thighs.

When she'd settled between them, her expression lost a little uncertainty. A determined gleam entered her eyes.

She bent over him, her bottom lifting into the air, and Brand wished he could be in two places at the same time because he'd love to see her from that angle, too.

But a soft hand cupped his balls, and suddenly he couldn't think of anything but the warmth of her fingers gliding over his sac.

She leaned closer, her breath licking his groin.

His balls tightened, pulling snug against his body.

A soft murmur escaped her, and then she opened wide and sucked one stone into her hot, wet mouth.

Brand's legs went rigid. His belly tightened. He speared his fingers through her hair and cupped her skull, tugging her closer while his semiflaccid cock throbbed.

She mouthed him gently, shielding the sharp edge of her teeth behind her lips, working her tongue over and over the orb, stroking him until he was nearly mindless and blood surged between his legs.

Her mouth widened, and she sucked the other inside, laving both balls now with broad strokes, tracing a fingernail beneath them along the sensitive skin leading toward his asshole.

It was his turn to get worried about her direction. Half of him wanted to know how far she'd dare go, the other half, the manly part of him, wanted to growl like a bear and drag her hand away.

In the end, she shyly fingered his asshole, not daring to enter, simply teasing him with wet, sliding circles that tickled his nerves to the point his cock straightened from where it had curved against his belly, filling and lifting, pulsing upward.

Begging for attention the way he would shortly if she didn't bring her mouth up his cock.

He tugged her hair, urging her higher.

Lyssa's mouth tightened around him. He suspected she smiled, knowing exactly the reaction she caused.

"Lyss, goddamn," he groaned. "My dick's so hard I'm gonna burst. Suck it, sweetheart."

She released his balls, gave them several short licks, and then moved upward. Her fingers wrapped around him as she bent to run her tongue along his shaft, licking around the base, swirling upward, taking so much time to wet every inch, his toes curled.

He lifted his knees, planted his heels into the mattress to lift his ass, and slid his shaft along her tongue. Then he gripped both sides of her head and guided her over the tip, not easing his hold until her mouth swallowed his crown.

Only then did he ease back. His breaths were shallow and ragged. His heart thudded so hard he could hear the beats in his ears, feel the pulse at his temples.

Lyssa gripped his cock and lowered her head, taking him deeper into her mouth, suctioning hard as she came up, releasing as she dove down.

His cock tapped the back of her throat, and she paused and then swallowed, her throat clasping his head in the sexiest caress imaginable and then opening, relaxing so she could slide on deeper.

She bobbed up and down, her tongue lapping at the sides of his shaft as her lips worked him, the suctioning growing stronger, her grip tightening, twisting, until his balls hardened like stones and he knew he was close to exploding.

He didn't want to come in her mouth. Not this time. He wanted *her* arousal coating his tongue.

Fisting his hand in her hair, he pulled her up, ignoring her murmured protests, pulling her up his body until her mouth slid over his.

Then he rolled, taking her beneath him, shifting his hips to the side to evade her seeking cunt. Rising over her, he forced her to her belly, snagged a pillow from the top of the bed and stuffed it under her hips. Then he pushed another beneath her to raise her ass higher.

Her face burrowed into the bedding, but she didn't try to fight him. When his hands urged her thighs apart, she didn't resist that either.

At last, he could see her glistening sex, the lips reddened and swollen. He nudged her thighs even wider, exposing her little asshole. His hands went to her buttocks, and he squeezed them, lifting them up and down, together and apart, massaging to soothe her unease.

Her thighs flexed, her bottom tilted higher, her invitation clear. She wanted to be fucked. Wanted his cock slamming deep into her cunt.

Soon enough, he wouldn't hold back a moment longer.

First, however, he had to remind her why she was here.

6

Lyssa's skin dimpled in goose bumps, and her body trembled anew as she wondered what he'd do next. She hoped he'd enter her quickly.

Sucking him off had been incredibly arousing. Feeling the tension enter his legs, his growing girth stretch her mouth— she'd had him at her mercy for at least a few moments.

Now she was at his. *Again.*

Not that she'd complain. Unless he made her wait too long.

Already her pussy spasmed, making embarrassingly succulent sounds she couldn't control. The involuntary caresses were a clear message she was ready—his for the taking.

Completely, drenchingly aroused.

The bed shifted behind her as he moved closer. The soft hairs clothing his legs brushed the insides of her calves, followed by another set of nudges that demanded she open wider.

So spread now she'd lost leverage, she leaned forward on her arms, waiting while his hands settled on her ass.

His palms were hot, his fingers splaying wide.

What was he doing? *Looking?* He'd said men liked to do that, but, *Jesus,* it was unnerving.

Without being able to read the changes in his expressions, she had to follow his commands, his *nudges,* to know what he wanted. And following direction had always been a problem for her. Especially when coming from him.

"Are you just gonna look?" she muttered, finally tired of trying to outwait him.

One hand lifted. She held her breath, her bottom and thighs tensing. Fingers dipped inside her vagina, turning, knuckles scraping.

Involuntarily she tightened around him, moistly clasping. *How many?* she wondered. Two? Thick, but not nearly what she needed.

Another finger fitted into her opening, stretching her deliciously, stroking in just a few inches. Not deep enough. She pulsed her hips, trying to lengthen the shallow thrusts.

Brand slid in and out, the tempo measured and steady.

Lyssa muzzled her next complaint against the coverlet, not wanting to give him the satisfaction of hearing her beg. Instead she held her breath and body still, determined not to give him a single clue he was quickly driving her out of her mind with want.

The fingers pulled free. His wet hand slid over one globe of her ass, leaving a sticky trail.

She didn't care. "Why'd you sto—" Her question was cut short by a sharp slap.

Before she could issue a screech, another stinging slap landed—and she forgot what she'd been about to say.

Left breathless from shock, smarting from his stinging abuse, she quivered on the pillow, her body arching hard, her bottom shimmying, dipping, trying to escape his hard hand.

Thwack!

"Bastard!" she finally issued in a garbled scream.

Thwack!

Her body understood before she did—accepted his punishment before her mind could wrap itself around the fact he spanked her like a child.

Her pussy softened, spilling arousal in a trickle that wet her labia and trailed down a thigh.

When the tips of his fingers spanked her wet pussy, tension exploded inside her, forcing from her a high-pitched howl of frustrated rage.

How did he know she craved his violence? Had that last slap against her sex been an accident?

Another slap landed directly on her swollen cunt, banging her hardening clit. Arousal spiked, sharp and jagged. Her hands clenched the bedding, and she rubbed her breasts against the nubby coverlet, seeking more stimulation, a softer abrasion to accompany the harsh stings warming her ass and pussy.

Before long, she writhed mindlessly, her knees trembling hard, her breaths shuddering through her.

When his hands rested on her hot skin, she sobbed, torn between the urge to beg for more and to pray he'd take her now.

Desire curled so tight it cramped her belly. She'd explode, come unglued the moment he entered her.

Brand's body blanketed her back, his cock slipping between her legs to glide lengthwise along her slit.

A wet kiss pressed against the back of her neck, and then his face nuzzled the corner of her neck. "Do you know what this is about, sweetheart?" he asked, his voice tight yet soft.

So soft, she trembled with misgivings. "You're punishing me?" she asked in a small voice, hating how young and vulnerable she sounded.

"I'm teaching you."

"What am I supposed to learn from this?" she bit out.

"That you shouldn't challenge me when I'm angry. Shouldn't tease me to the point I lose it."

"This about Cody?"

"I told you not to say his name. But that's not it either."

"You want me obedient?" she asked, her voice firming, true anger beginning to flush through her.

"In most things."

"I'm not like that. You know me."

A deep breath filled the chest draping over her back. Firm kisses dotted her shoulder and the corner of her neck. "I think you are. You challenge me at every turn. It's deliberate. Sometimes dangerous." Teeth scraped up the side of her neck. "It stops now," he whispered in her ear.

She gasped as a quiver bit the back of her neck and traveled down her spine. "Or what?"

His tongue lapped the curve of her earlobe. "We do this again."

Her breathless huff sounded weak, even to her own ears, and she tilted her head. "That's supposed to deter me? You couldn't tell how much I loved it?"

Brand's body snuggled closer, his arms wrapping around her torso. "Next time, I won't finish it."

"What do you mean?" she asked, her mind not functioning well with his hands sending luscious sensations shooting straight to her brain, seeming to short-circuit her intellect.

Then his body grew still. The grip of his hands loosened.

It took a moment for his message to get through. "You mean you won't give me satisfaction . . . like you're going to now?" she finished hopefully.

"Exactly."

Annoyance and pride prodded her to struggle inside his embrace. She tried to close her legs, to creep forward on the mattress, but found it impossible to wriggle away. "I can't promise obedience, Brand. I won't."

"I'm not asking for obedience in everything. Just where your safety and your sweet cunt are concerned." His cock prodded between her legs for emphasis.

Moisture greeted him, her entrance spasming as it tried to suck him deep. With his hands closing around her breasts, all she could do was stretch, her back arching.

Let him think she tried to escape, but really she needed the coverlet scouring her skin every place he didn't touch. She felt on fire. "You say that like you plan to keep me."

"I don't share," he said, his tone deepening into a delightful growl. His cock tapped her sex again, pulled away, and then came back, sinking the tip inside.

A tiny, mewling moan escaped with her next breath. "That sounds awfully like you're laying a claim."

"I placed my brand right on your ass," he said, pushing the thick, blunt tip a little deeper.

Her cunt throbbed, and she groaned. "Maybe that's one promise I can keep . . . saving this pussy just for you. But you gotta keep me busy . . . too busy to think about stepping out of line."

"I think I can keep up. Don't you?"

A breathy laugh gusted from her. "*Sweet fuck.* I'm so hot I hurt."

"You're gonna have bruises on your ass. Know that?"

"I don't mind. Just finish it."

His hips dipped away, his cock sliding out, down her folds, and then coming back to prod between them.

She sucked in a ragged breath. "I want it hard."

"So do I. Better hold tight."

That was all the warning he gave before his hips jerked forward, impaling her with his hard-as-stone rod.

A choked sob racked her. As he leaned away from her back, she gathered her knees under her, bracing for a violent flurry.

Brand didn't disappoint.

His hands clasping her warm ass, he pounded into her, thrusting so hard his groin slapped against her moist sex.

Lyssa rolled her face in the bedding, breathing hard, her body already beginning to convulse.

His hands slid to the notches of her hips, holding her still as he hammered harder, faster, his shaft heating up her passage as he rammed deeper, tunneling into her, the end of every thrust digging sharply upward.

The tension built inside her until it exploded, and her back arched, a howl ripping from her throat as light exploded behind her tightly squeezed eyelids.

Still, his furious fucking didn't ease, didn't slow. His strokes grew uneven, frantic. His breaths ended on soft grunts. His fingers bit into her flesh. He pulled her hips to his in violent, frenzied jounces until, at last, she felt a hot jet of cum spill into her womb.

At that moment, she realized they'd forgotten the condom.

The fact must have registered with him, too. "*Fuck. Goddamnit.*" He fell over her, his hips still rocking. His arms slid along her sides, gliding under her torso. His head landed on her uninjured shoulder. "Jesus, Lyss."

She waited, gasping for breath as his weight pressed her deep into the mattress. The shudders vibrating his large frame soothed her.

When he pulled out his slick cock, his arms withdrew as well, and he rolled to his back. He covered his eyes with a forearm.

Lyssa dragged the pillows from under her hips and lay on her side, facing him. Waiting for him to meet her gaze.

A deep sigh billowed his cheeks, and he thrust his arm beneath his head to raise it before turning his face toward hers. "I'm sorry."

She gave a little careless shrug. "Is it so bad? I know I'm clean."

His gaze slid away. "I didn't take care of you."

She reached out and smoothed her hand over his chest, combing dark hairs that curled lovingly around her fingertips. "But you will. If it's necessary."

A tender light entered his eyes. The same look he'd given her when he'd knelt beside her when he'd freed her from the barbed wire. She recognized it now for what it was. Love. Brand loved her.

A deep swallow worked the muscles of his neck. "Come here," he said hoarsely.

For the first time, she didn't mask her reaction with a quip or a defensive snarl. Eagerly she snuggled close, resting her head on his shoulders.

His lips pressed a soft kiss to her forehead.

"Would it really be so bad?" she asked softly, needing to know if her instincts were right.

His free hand cupped her chin, tilting her head up. Their gazes met and held. Warmth filled her at the crooked smile that curved his lips. "Think we should try it that way again? Just to make sure we have a reason to worry?"

Her lips stretched even though she felt sure the tears filling her eyes and the tremble of her lips were going to disintegrate any moment into a truly soppy cry. She took a deep, shuddering breath. "No going back?" she asked, echoing his words.

He shook his head. "I think I've just been waiting."

"For what?"

"For you to be old enough to know your own mind."

A tear slid down her cheek as she decided to suck up her courage. "I've known I loved you since I was a little girl. What took you so long?"

He winced; then his lips tightened in a sad smile. "You're gonna have to teach me how to be a family man. I didn't have the best examples."

Lyssa narrowed her eyes. "I swear sometimes you're a complete idiot."

A dark brow lifted, challenging her to continue.

"You take care of everyone. Riding herd on me, on Danny. I know you did it out of love. It's what family does."

She reached out to smooth a hand over his chest before continuing more carefully. "So your mom and dad let you down. You didn't use their abandonment to give you an excuse to give up. You've kept the ranch going, provided a roof for Danny as he grew. Meddled in his business and mine until we're both bucking to let you know we're ready to ride on our own."

"Is that what you need now? Freedom?"

Lyssa rolled her eyes and huffed out a breath. Then her gaze slid away as she mustered the courage for one more truth. "I've fought you every step of the way because I wanted to break through with you. Wanted you to lose control." A quick glance at his face, and she saw tension enter his features and his eyes darken with passion. "I challenge you because it turns me on. And I hope it does the same for you." She swallowed and waited, hoping she hadn't laid too much of her heart bare for him to tromp right over. If she'd misread him, if he didn't feel the same about her . . .

Brand moved so quick she blinked, and suddenly she was beneath him. "Are you always going to buck my authority?"

"I don't think I can stop myself. I think it's genetics."

"The red hair?"

She nodded, her throat so tight and full she couldn't push another word past it.

"Did you mean it when you said you loved me? Do you still?"

Again she nodded.

He swooped down for a quick, hard kiss and then lifted his head again. "I want your sweet body under me, your pussy swallowing me whole every goddamn night. I want you here in the morning, waking up beside me."

Sure sounded like love. But could he say the words?

Determined not to be disappointed, she reminded herself he was a man and naturally averse to sentiment—and completely clueless when putting feelings into words.

With his cock quickly filling, pushing against her folds, her arousal bloomed. Her nipples tightened, beading against his furred chest. Her swollen pussy caressed his cock with a ridiculously moist welcome.

His mouth hovered just above hers. The intensity of his gaze seared her. "I wanna make babies with you, Lyss."

Damn, that sounded good enough. She licked her lips. "Mac's gonna have your ass if you don't marry me first."

"I was getting there."

She lifted both eyebrows. "Really?"

"You're always quick to jump ahead," he said, his tone sliding like silk.

"Guess you're gonna have to teach me patience along with obedience." His mouth stretched into a smile so full of masculine confidence her toes curled.

"Like your lessons so far?" he rasped.

"Bet I won't be able to sit easy for a week."

"I'll have to keep you on your back then." His smile slipped. "You're marrying me, right?"

Feeling her own confidence soar, she arched one eyebrow.

67

"Oh, I don't know. That wasn't the most romantic proposal a woman could ever hope for."

"Did I screw it up?"

Soft laughter bubbled up inside her. "It was perfect. The fact your dick is pushing inside me is something I won't mention to our kids when they ask for the story."

He winced. "Guess I'll have to do it again—for posterity."

"I'll expect roses."

"Didn't know you were the flowers kind of girl."

"Don't know everything about me, do you?"

His gaze narrowed as he thrust deeper. "I think I know most of the important things."

"Oh? Like?"

"How to get you so hot you'll do anything. Promise me anything."

"There is that. Did you learn anything else?"

"Hmmm . . . I know how you sound when you come."

"I make sounds?" she gasped as he made a sexy little side-to-side motion that stretched her.

"Just like a hungry little kitten."

She wrinkled her nose. "So now I'm cute and fluffy?"

"Does make me want to stroke your fur. It's sexy as hell." Several shallow strokes, building on each other, caused a ripple of inner muscles that caressed the length of his shaft.

They both gasped.

"Guess that's not so bad," she said, trying to catch a breath. "Anything else?"

A low growl rumbled through his chest. "I think I found your G-spot."

Another gust of laughter escaped her. "You even know what that is?"

His eyes narrowed. "I may spend most of my days ridin' a horse, but I do know my way around a woman's body."

"Think you know where it is?"

He shifted on the mattress. "I'm grazing it now, aren't I? Your eyes just got that smoky look."

Her hips rolled upward, taking him deeper, helping him angle his cock just right. "Cowboy, do it again."

Brand rose on his arms and tunneled inside, circling his hips as he drove deeper. His jaws clamped shut, and muscles rippled along his shoulders and biceps as he rocked hard against her.

Lyssa wrapped her arms around him, lifted her legs to ride his narrow hips, and gave herself over to his mastery. So, he hadn't said he loved her, but he was certainly attentive to her pleasure.

Good enough for now.

7

Lyssa squinted at the sky from beneath the brim of her cowboy hat. A turkey buzzard circled in the distance, its black, ragged-edged wings stretching to scrape the wide blue sky.

The heavy clouds keeping the weather unseasonably cool the past few days had been swept away during the night when the winds changed course from the Gulf and drier air blew in from the north. Heat intensified as the sun slid higher in the sky, promising a scorcher of day.

Not too hot for a picnic just yet.

The thought made her smile. An action she'd been repeating all morning long. Her ranch foreman, Santiago, had been giving her quizzical looks, making her wonder if she usually rode around with a sour expression on her face. Or whether he could see the pink surrounding her mouth—whisker-burn she'd done her best to hide with a little foundation.

Maybe the makeup made him wonder. Most days she never bothered.

Another glance at the sky had her sighing. They'd been looking for stray cattle, so Lyssa pulled the reins to the side and gave her horse a nudge to follow the scavenging bird.

Santiago, who rode on the opposite side of the small herd of lowing cattle they'd gathered, lifted his chin in question.

She pointed upward, held up her hand with all fingers spread to indicate she'd only be gone for five, and left him and the cattle behind.

They'd been riding in and out of gullies all morning, retrieving bawling calves. The buzzard hovered above another dry creek. She hoped she wasn't already too late.

The hard work was welcome, keeping her mind off the anticipation humming through her. Brand had promised to meet her later for lunch—a picnic on a hilltop between both ranches. A surprisingly romantic gesture after the too efficient way he'd hustled her out of his house in the early morning hours.

He'd set an alarm, waking her with a gentle shake after letting the shower run long enough to heat the water to just the right temperature. He'd held a towel and cup of steaming coffee when she stepped out.

She'd hoped for at least a kiss, but he'd dressed quietly and waited for her at the door. Dressed in his customary blue work shirt and jeans, her heart did a little flip-flop at the sight of him.

Now she knew exactly what the chambray and denim hid.

How she would have loved smoothing her hands around his trim waist and leaning close to nuzzle his neck, just to breath in his scent, but he seemed remote, a different man from the one who'd loved her with a wild, unrestricted roughness throughout the night.

Wondering if he was having morning-after regrets, she'd bit her tongue and followed him out, remaining quiet until he'd pulled his truck up in front her home.

Then, feeling awkward and disappointed, she yanked on the

71

door handle, only to pause when his fingers wrapped around her forearm.

He'd leaned toward her, pressed a quick kiss to her lips, and issued the invitation, his dark eyes filling with their own brand of smoky desire.

"Thought you were giving me a brush-off," she whispered when they drew apart.

His masculine grimace did a lot to dispel her doubts. "Had to get you out of my bed quick," he said in low, growling rasp.

Lyssa tilted her head, glancing up from beneath her eyelashes. "Why's that?"

"I woke up before you did. Watched you sleeping."

Her lips twitched. "Did I snore? Drool?"

He cleared his throat, and a faint grin curved the corners of his lips. "Just a little. Knew if I didn't get moving right away I'd keep you there all day."

His words melted her irritation. Lyssa decided to forgive him. "Not so bad, was it? Sleeping with me?"

An indrawn breath lifted his deep chest. "Pure hell. I feel as ornery as an old mule right now."

Lyssa lifted an eyebrow and slid her hand up his thigh. "Cowboy, I wouldn't have minded helping you take the edge off."

His hand closed over hers, halting her just short of her destination. "You ready to announce to the world you're steppin' out with me?"

"Why not? I think it's a little late to keep it a secret." She pointed a finger over her shoulder. "Juanita's probably got her nose pressed to the window."

"Let's give her a little more to gossip about." He pulled her across the leather seat, and a thickly muscled arm swept her close for a kiss that stole what was left of her breath.

When they both came up for air, Brand kissed her forehead and let her go. "See you later. Keep an eye out for trouble."

"Yes, sir," she said with just enough starch to remind him she remembered her lessons.

Heat banked in his brown eyes. "Think you'll be able to sit on a horse?"

She snorted. "I'm a Texas girl. I can ride all day and night."

His lips stretched wider, and he shook his head. "Get out of here. Quick."

The memory of his expression, at once amused and pained, had kept her smiling to herself.

At that moment, she'd known exactly how he felt: aroused and wishing he hadn't been so quick to leave his bed. But he'd probably anticipated exactly how uncomfortable she'd grow in the passing hours and thought it a just "punishment."

Sliding into her saddle that morning hadn't been something she could take for granted. She'd lost count how many times she stood in her stirrups to ease the delicious ache between her legs. An ache intensified with each jounce of her tender bottom against the hard leather saddle.

Perhaps she'd let him rub the hurt away during their "picnic."

Gravel scraping down the side of an embankment drew her attention.

She clucked at her horse, tapped his flanks, and entered a copse of mesquite and tall buffalo grass that rimmed the edge of the steep-banked creek. Careful of tall prickly pear cacti, she wove through the vegetation, searching the embankment until she found an eroded edge and steered her horse into the arroyo.

Her first indication that something wasn't right was the tension in the horse's neck as he fought the bit and snorted. Then his ears pricked forward, and he started to back up. But with his hooves already sliding in caliche, it was too late.

From around a bend at the bottom of the deep, dry creek, two men stepped out, pistols pointing in her direction.

"So, big brother, was that really little Lyssa McDonough I saw you hustling into your pickup this morning?"

Brand gritted his teeth at his brother's cheerfully drawled comment. "Don't you have anything better to do right now? Like get your résumé ready?"

"Just trying to get my mind around it," Danny said, a wicked grin sliding across his lips. "You and Lyss. Who'd-a thought?"

Discussing Lyssa with his little brother wasn't something Brand was willing to do. The memories of how he'd spent his time with her were still too sweet, too raw. "Why aren't you ridin' herd on the other side of the fence today?" he muttered. "The McDonoughs hardly need us both over here."

Danny sat relaxed in his saddle, his gaze following the rutted trail along the fence line. "Thought you might like the company." He flashed Brand a teasing glance. "You look a little worse for wear. Gettin' a little old for an all-nighter?"

Brand cut him a blistering sideways glance. "We're not talkin' about this."

Danny's brown eyes danced with ill-concealed humor. "Am I supposed to pretend I didn't hear a whole lot of commotion coming from your bedroom last night?"

"Thought you would have stayed a little longer in town," Brand growled.

"I did. How was I supposed to know you'd just be gettin' started when I rolled in?"

"Danny . . ." Brand pushed his lips together.

Soft laughter shook his brother's shoulders. "Can't help it. It's too damn funny. You should see your face. You look ready to spit nails—and you're blushing."

"I don't blush."

"Sure you don't. And you're not so eager to see her again you're makin' up excuses to ride her side of the fence."

"I don't need an excuse. I'm just checkin' up on her, like Mac asked."

"Yeah, good ol' Mac. . . ." Danny waggled his eyebrows. "Wonder what he's gonna say—"

"Do you want me to pull you out of your saddle and beat that smile off your face?"

Danny lifted his hands in mock surrender. "All right, I'll lay off." Only a moment passed before he turned in his saddle again. "But I don't think Mac will have a problem with it. He'll know for sure Lyssa trapped you good."

Brand gave him a sharp glance, wanting to ask what he meant but still irritated enough to not want the conversation continuing.

Danny shrugged. "Mac knew before he left that askin' you that favor would put you squarely in her path. She's his sister— he wants her happy. You're his best friend. He'll want to knock the shit out of you when he sees you, but he'll still be glad you're part of the family."

"You couldn't have clued me in earlier he had an ulterior motive?"

"And spoil the fun? He wants all the details, by the way."

"Some things he's best not ever knowin'."

"Oh, I don't know. He'd probably give you a medal for the spankin'."

Brand issued a low, vicious curse, but Danny kicked his horse into a gallop, laughing as he pulled ahead.

They left the grassy plain, heading toward a line of mesquite and cedar trees along a creek. They saw the dust rising before they found the cattle herd and a lone cowboy.

"Santiago!" Danny called out. "Hola, amigo. *Qué pasó!*"

Brand cast a glance around, knowing Santiago was supposed to be shadowing Lyssa that day. "*Dónde está* Lyssa?"

Santiago shrugged. "She left a little while ago. Gone into the creek looking for more *vacas*. Grass is drying out. We have fresh hay and need to keep them together."

"Which way?" Brand asked.

Santiago pointed, and Brand didn't wait to extend more pleasantries. Lyssa knew she shouldn't be alone.

Danny caught him before he reached the stand of trees. "From the scowl on your face, looks like the honeymoon's already over."

"She's reckless. Damn stupid when it comes to her own safety."

"She's competent. Been on a horse as long as I have."

Brand's fist ached from clenching the reins. "There have been signs of intrusion all over this spread. A little caution isn't too much to ask."

"Did you ever do that? Ask? Or did you just tell her how it would be?"

Brand's lips firmed into a stubborn line. "Have you ever tried to reason with that woman?"

"That why you spanked her? Trying to get the message branded on her sweet little ass?" Danny's eyes gleamed with wicked amusement. "Doesn't look like the lesson took. Might need to repeat it. 'Course, I'm not sure how Mac will feel about you turning her over your knee."

Brand listened, but his attention snagged on signs pressed into the dirt. He leaned forward in his saddle to study footprints in the sandy soil.

Though he was no trained tracker, he could still tell that a couple of individuals had passed through here on foot.

Mules, then. He'd been right. Drug runners had cut across

her property on their way toward some pickup along the highway farther north.

Brand held up his hand for silence and drew back on his reins. "Did you hear that?" he whispered.

Danny shook his head, but his expression tightened, and he cocked his ear toward the arroyo.

Brand pulled his rifle from its scabbard and dismounted. "I heard scuffling." He crept toward the edge and then knelt in the tall, dried grass to peer into the gulley.

What he saw caused his heart to clench in his chest.

Three people were in the center of the creek bed. There were two men, one older and with a stocky build, the other much younger, maybe in his late teens. Both wore bulging packs strapped to their backs.

Both held weapons.

Lyssa knelt on her knees in front of them, her head bowed and hands tied behind her back.

The older man stood behind her, arguing with his companion, his gun jerking in the air to emphasize his fury.

Danny settled beside him on his belly, pushing aside tall blades of grass with the barrel of his rifle to get a look. "I tied the horses off," he whispered.

Brand breathed deeply to slow his heart's frantic pounding and lifted his gun and set the stock firmly against his shoulder.

Staring through the sights, he ignored the sweat rolling down his forehead, stinging his eyes, and watched, waiting to see how this would play out. Hoping like hell for an opening that would put the men far enough away from Lyssa that he wouldn't risk hitting her by accident or getting her shot by one of the armed men once they realized they weren't alone.

He saw Lyssa lift her head and her lips move.

The one standing behind her slammed the hand holding the pistol against her shoulder. She fell sideways to the dirt.

"Fucking bastard," Danny spat furiously beside him, rising on his elbows to point his weapon toward the men menacing Lyssa.

Brand's whole body tightened with rage. His forefinger slid around the front of the trigger.

Lyssa struggled up from the ground, shooting a frightened glance over her shoulder at the raging man. Her lips worked again.

Damnit, Lyssa. You don't argue with a man holding a gun!

He forced his gaze from Lyssa's pale, stark face to the man who threatened her life. The man's expression was cold, set, his black eyes unwavering in their intent. He wouldn't risk leaving a witness. His arm lifted, raising the nozzle of his handgun.

Lyssa's body stiffened, and she faced away, her eyes squeezing shut.

Brand sighted down the barrel of his weapon, fighting the tremor working through his belly. He had to get this right, couldn't lose her now to a blown shot.

Before the man had finished lifting the barrel to point it at the back of her bent head, Brand pulled back the trigger and prayed.

8

Lyssa heard the loud report and jerked. But no searing pain from a bullet ripped through her. Something thudded heavily to the dirt behind her. Footsteps scraped and fell fast as they sped away.

Shaking uncontrollably, her ears buzzing, she opened her eyes, turning slowly to look behind her, and gagged at the sight of her attacker, his head split open by a gaping wound that bled quickly into the sandy creek bed.

Gravel scraped in a rocky fall of skittering pebbles, and suddenly a pair of long, leather chaps appeared before her.

She lifted her head, swaying on her knees, staring up through eyes so filled with tears she had to blink to clear them before she saw it was Brand, a rifle still gripped inside his fist.

He tossed away the weapon, dropped to his knees in front of her, and opened his arms.

Lyssa fell against his chest, her teeth chattering, sinking her forehead against his shoulder while his arms closed around her and squeezed away her breath.

For long moments they stayed like that, Brand gripping her tightly against his chest, rocking slowly forward and back.

The buzzing in her head quieted to be replaced with Brand's softly murmured words. "Baby, you okay? Did they hurt you?" His hands smoothed up and down her back and then cupped the back of her head as though seeking to reassure himself.

A ragged sob trembled through her, and she burrowed deeper against him, so grateful he'd found her she couldn't speak. She shook her head.

"Shhh. I've got you. It's over now," he cooed; then he cleared his throat. "Danny, move him." Brand's hands continued to glide up and down her back. His cheek settled against the top of her head, and he rocked with her.

Scraping behind her didn't startle her. She knew Danny was moving the body, and she didn't bother to look. She didn't need to add one more horror to her memory of today.

Instead she cried, letting Brand soothe her and himself, she suspected, from the soft shudders that shook beneath her cheek.

Fingers enclosed hers, squeezing gently, and then tugged at the ropes behind her. Finally free, she moaned as blood rushed back into her hands. She slowly brought them forward and wrapped her arms around Brand's strong body.

"What did I tell you, baby girl?" he whispered into her hair.

"Gonna start on me now?" she grumbled.

A soft snort sounded behind her.

"Danny, get back to Santiago. Have him go back to call for the sheriff."

"You got things handled here, brother?"

Brand's head lifted from hers. "I'll bring her with me. We won't be far behind you."

"That other bastard's long gone."

"He might still backtrack to get his pack."

"Fuck, guess I'll have to take it with me."

Several minutes passed before Lyssa felt strong enough to lean away. She gazed up into Brand's face and shivered at what she saw there. Anger so dark and lethal she had to glance away. "I'm sorry. I didn't see them coming until it was too late. Thought I was chasing a calf."

"Can you get on your feet?" he asked, his tone flat.

She nodded, feeling her mouth tremble. With his hands under her elbows, she stood, catching herself when she began to teeter again.

An arm curved around her waist, and she let him turn her toward the embankment.

"Can you make it?"

Her chin came up. "I'm not hurt," she bit out.

"You will be," came his low, growled promise.

Startled, she swung back to look at his face.

His narrowed gaze burnished every place it landed. Her eyes, her lips.

Her mouth parted. "Brand . . . ?"

His head shook, a fierce anger flooding his pale cheeks with color, his expression etched in sharp fury.

She shrugged off his arm and stumbled to the bank, crawling up on her hands and knees until she stood in the grass and the sunshine beat down on her unprotected face.

Closing her eyes, she lifted her head, ignoring him as he climbed up beside her. How could she blame him for his anger? She'd been careless. Hadn't believed his warnings. She'd always had confidence she could handle herself in just about any situation, but she'd been caught flat-footed with this one.

Now a man lay dead in the gulley below. The man she loved looked ready to strangle her he was so furious.

How could things have gone awry so fast?

"Let's go."

She trudged behind him as he retrieved his horse.

"I should find my mount," she said softly.

"Let your men do that. I'm getting you back to the house."

His words, issued in bulleted gusts, angered her. "Wait a second. Do you think anyone else would have been more prepared than I was for what went down?"

"You shouldn't have been alone."

"I was doing my job. Same as Santiago. It could have been him walking into an ambush."

"Well, it wasn't. Get your ass on this horse."

Blood pumped in her ears. "*Fuck you.* I'll walk back." She turned and stomped a few steps in the direction she'd left her cattle and foreman, only to be dragged back by an arm snaking around her middle.

Brand brought her up hard against his chest. "Don't . . . fight me. Not now."

"Why not? Feels damn good." Her chin notched higher. "Pretty goddamn normal, don't you think? You're telling me what to do again—I'm telling you to go to hell."

Brand's hand clamped on her forearm, and he turned her, pulling her in, his legs bracing apart as he grabbed her bottom and forced her hips closer to his.

A thick ridge pressed into her belly. "We're going home. Now."

Lyssa's mouth dropped open to deliver another quick retort, but his tight-lipped fury, combined with the jut of his rigid sex digging into her, melted her resistance. She nodded dumbly, let him turn her away, and didn't even complain when he gave her a gentle shove forward.

Strength returned to her legs as a stirring of sensual excitement lit a slow-burning fire in her gut.

Once again he sat her sideways on his horse, forcing her head against his shoulder before taking up the reins and turning the horse toward home.

They barely made it to his bedroom, fighting each other to strip away their clothing. Managing to get their boots and pants off but cursing at their shirts, leaving them hanging at their elbows before they fell across the mattress in a sprawl of limbs.

When he thrust inside, a cry tore from her throat.

Brand turned his head and kissed her cheek. "I know, baby. I know." He powered in, driving straight up, not stopping until his cock was swallowed whole.

Lyssa groaned and wound her legs tightly around his waist. "Didn't know if I'd be here again, you inside me—"

"Damn near killed me—"

"Christ, don't slow down," she said—urgent, agonizing need curling around her womb as Brand thrust rapidly, powering into her. "What about . . . sheriff?" she gasped.

"Danny . . . has better sense," he gritted out, slamming his mouth over hers as his strokes shortened, sharpened, tunneling so deep she knew neither of them would last long.

The first spiraling ripples hit her so fast she half groaned, half laughed and let go, following him to the edge of ecstasy, before tumbling headfirst. Her whole body spasmed, her vagina clamping hard around his cock.

"Lysssss . . ." he groaned, his movements growing jerky, desperate.

She raised her hands and framed his cheeks, staring into his face as the moment hit him.

His eyes closed, his lips pulled away from his teeth in a feral grimace. Then cum jetted inside her in scalding spurts.

As he slowed the movement of his hips, lapping gently inside her, she pressed kisses to his neck, his jaw, at last kissing his mouth.

Their lips glided together and apart as he continued to rock against her. "Don't want it to end. God . . . feels incredible."

She kissed him again and then settled back, feasting her eyes on him. How incredibly beautiful he was—the sharp edge of his jaw grinding hard, his brown eyes locking with her gaze as if he couldn't look away.

"I love you, Lyss," he said, his voice rough as sandpaper.

Her eyes filled, blurring his features. "I love you, too."

"Don't ever do that to me again."

Another quick kiss, and she nodded, nuzzling his neck as he settled atop her body, surrounding her completely.

A knock sounded at the bedroom door.

Brand sighed and turned to shout over his shoulder, "Be out in a few minutes." Turning back to her, he gave her a crooked smile. "Thought Danny would stall them a little longer."

"When did you have a chance to arrange this with him?"

"Didn't have to."

She arched one eyebrow. "One of those guy things? Danger over, knees no longer wobbling, gotta have sex?"

"My knees never wobbled. Woman, anyone ever tell you you've got a smart mouth?"

"You. More times than I can count." She grinned slowly, warmth spreading through her chest as his lips finally relaxed and slipped into a sexy smile.

"Did you mean it?" she asked softly.

"Every word. All three."

"Think Mac will approve?"

"Wishing he were here?"

She nodded, hoping she wasn't about to dissolve into tears again. But her heart felt so full.

He turned his head to kiss her open palm before looking down again. "I think Mac expected this to happen."

"Smart man, my brother."

"Want to wait until he's back to get married?"

Her eyes opened wide. "Are you kidding? And live in sin until he gets here? He'll kick your ass."

"Soon as we get a license, then."

Again she nodded. With her breaths evening, slowing, she began to smooth her hands over his shoulders, his back, loving the hard, unforgiving strength of his lean, muscled frame. "What must Danny be thinking?"

"That I'm damn lucky to have you." His jaw flexed. A swallow rippled along his throat. "You okay? No bad moments?"

Lyssa shook her head and hugged him one last time and then let him go. As he rolled from the bed and picked up the clothes from the floor, Lyssa knew she was the lucky one.

"Tell me," he said, buttoning his shirt, "were you tellin' me the truth when you said any man would do?"

She narrowed her eyes, giving his body a sexy once-over. "Any man who just happens to live on the ranch next door."

The corners of his lips tipped upward. "You could have gone for Danny."

She wrinkled her nose. "Too young. I prefer a man with enough experience to know his way around a woman's body."

A grin tugged at his lips. "Narrows it down a bit but there could still be a couple of hands who fit that description," he said, finishing the buttons on his cuffs.

"Hmmm . . ." she said, pretending to consider it. "They don't make me weak just looking at them."

A look of pure male satisfaction darkened his features. "I do that?"

She nodded and strolled slowly toward him. "They don't make me almost come with their mouth on my breasts."

"I'll have to try harder later."

She reached up and closed a button near the top of his shirt before looking into his eyes. "They don't make me think about babies and forever." She paused and licked her lips. "That scare you? The babies part?"

"Not a bit. So long as every one of them's mine."

She tilted her head and gave him a saucy smile. "You probably figure a big belly is the best kind of brand."

"Uh-huh. But doesn't mean I won't want to give you a reminder or two about the rules later tonight."

Standing on tiptoe, she wrapped her arms around his shoulders. "Cowboy, I'm countin' on it."

Slow Ride

1

Sometimes destiny rushed up to meet a man head-on; sometimes he just had to take a step backward.

Daniel Tynan raised his arms to stretch his back, wincing at a twinge in a muscle behind his shoulder. Although accustomed to physical labor, he'd overdone it today, but the effort had been well worth it.

Glancing out a window, he noted the darkness and raked his hand through his hair, grimacing when he pulled away pieces of straw. He'd dragged his feet long enough.

He picked his Stetson off the corner post of the last stall he'd cleaned and set it on top of his head. His first day at Wasp Creek Ranch had left him feeling deeply satisfied with his choice, despite the aches. He was needed here.

Seven years had passed since he'd spent a summer wrangling under Douglas Dermott's tutelage, learning how to work with the horses. Quarter horses for reining, cutting, and racing, as well as the occasional Appaloosa. Douglas had loved them all, had taken pride in his breeding program and shared his skill as a trainer with quiet patience.

A raw teenager, Danny had been eager to take on a new challenge—one not so far removed from his own upbringing on a cattle ranch that he'd felt completely out of his element.

He'd learned a lot from Douglas.

Too bad he'd returned the gift by lusting after the man's wife.

Even at the time, the irony of his situation hadn't escaped Danny. He'd lost his mother when she'd run off with a younger man, which made his own addiction all the more disturbing.

Days ago, when the job notice had appeared on Tara Toomey's bulletin board, he'd felt shaken, reminded of his indiscretion. Nevertheless, he'd been curious about the widow and how she'd fared since the death of her husband. He didn't question the urge that had him faxing an application to her foreman as soon as Brand had given him the green light to go.

Reggie Haskell remembered him, calling him the next day to offer him the job. Which had surprised him, given that Reggie had been all too aware of Danny's old obsession with "Miz Dermott."

However, it seemed the Dermott's ranch wasn't doing well, and the widow needed all the experienced help she could find to get horses ready for auction while she put the ranch up for sale.

Even beneath a darkening sky, Danny could see the subtle signs of distress. A barn that needed a coat of paint. Stalls not as meticulously kept as they should have been. A diminished herd—still prime horseflesh—but only a shadow of the animals Douglas had taken so much pride in introducing to a young man.

Without Douglas's leadership, the widow hadn't been able

to manage as well. Local banks didn't have confidence in her ability to keep the ranch in the red, hiking up the interest rates on the seasonal loans she'd needed to stay afloat.

That the entire county suffered under a long drought, forcing them to buy more hay to compensate for the fields of scorched grass they'd lost, had only added to her woes.

From Reggie, Danny had gotten a laundry list of the problems they'd faced in the last three years. While he'd listened, Danny's mind kept wandering back to Douglas's widow.

How heartbreaking to lose her husband and now face losing the ranch. Yet Danny couldn't stem the shameful rush of elation that swept through him when he thought of her—all alone, perhaps in need of a man's comfort.

Although no longer a gangly teen, he had no illusions that she might take an interest in him now. Seven years had passed, but another dozen or so still separated them in age. She'd given him a room inside her home rather than a rough cot in the mostly empty bunkhouse. The same room he'd stayed in the last time he'd been here.

She hadn't seen him as anything other than a boy then. Apparently she still didn't.

This time, he held a halfhearted wish he'd see her only as an attractive older woman. After all, he'd had more experience with the opposite sex since his younger days. Was more jaded where women were concerned, was less impressed with a fine figure and a pair of dewy brown eyes.

That wish bit the dust just before suppertime that day, when Danny had stood in the doorway of the barn, rubbing oil into the old saddle he'd brought with him. Though he hadn't bothered bringing a horse, preferring to travel light, he liked working with his own equipment. Besides, the saddle held sentimental value. It had been his father's and was the first saddle Danny had ever ridden.

From the corner of his eye, he'd watched the front door of the ranch house open. His hand had hovered over the leather as he'd gazed from the shadows at the woman who'd stepped onto the wide porch of the white, clapboard ranch house to shake out a throw rug, her body jerking in delicious little waves.

"You're not thinkin' about slidin' back into that old saddle, again, are ya?" Reggie muttered from behind him.

Danny glanced back and flashed the older man a smile, narrowing his eyes to warn him to mind his own damn business. "Maybe I'll just polish her up and take her for a ride."

Reggie shook his head. "A fine animal like that needs a firm hand and follow through. You give her too much rein, and you'll never get her to go where you want her to."

Without another word, Reggie led a mare from the barn, leaving Danny to wonder whether he'd been talking about the woman or the horse.

Reggie's words had stuck with him the rest of the day.

He'd worked steadily, mucking stalls, inventorying and tidying equipment he'd need in the coming days.

He headed back from the barn in the darkness, having purposely delayed the moment he had to face her.

He'd worried she might read his interest in his face. Or, worse, that he might give away his shame with a stammer or a blush—not that he did that much these days. But he remembered how easily she'd disarmed him, made him feel as though he had two left feet each time he fell under the spell of her soft brown gaze.

He'd stalled long enough. Missed dinner because he hadn't wanted to see her for the first time surrounded by a group of rowdy cowboys at the large kitchen table.

Needing to look his fill, unremarked by anyone else, he wanted to catch her unawares, note the changes close-up in her face and lush figure, and just maybe lay to rest the attraction that had burned through him the first time he'd laid eyes on her.

Lights blazed on the wide wraparound porch as he approached the house. One lit a back-room window.

Mostly hidden by a large live oak, he shouldn't have noted it. However, he remembered all too well the window belonged to her bathroom.

One he hadn't been able to resist peering inside seven years ago when he'd been a lonely teen, missing his parents and his older brother and lusting after a woman who didn't see him as anything more than a boy.

His steps slowed. He pulled a ragged pack of cigarettes from his pocket. He didn't smoke much, but right now he needed an excuse to linger outside.

He tamped a cigarette against the side of a finger, stuck the butt in his mouth, and lit the end, drawing deeply as he stared at the window with the slatted blinds and remembered.

Maggie Dermott had been everything a boy starving for a woman's attention could want.

The picture of her rounded figure, glossy brown hair and wide, doelike brown eyes still burned in his mind. The first time she'd turned her soft gaze on him and offered him a smile, she'd melted him all the way to his toes.

She'd been lovely. Soft and womanly. Smelled of roses and soap and freshly baked bread.

He'd had a lot of time to rationalize his obsession. He'd been close to his mother, missing her terribly when she'd abandoned them all, leaving him in the care of his father until he'd managed to drink himself to death.

Afterward, Brandon had kept the ranch afloat, providing a familiar roof over his head, but he'd had his own grief to deal with and a whole new set of responsibilities to keep him occupied.

Daniel had felt the loss of his mother most keenly. Still, he didn't think that totally explained his attraction to his boss's young wife.

Nor did it excuse the fact he'd watched her.

The night Danny had surrendered to her sensual appeal, Douglas had attended an out-of-town auction. Danny had walked from the barn, saw the light shining from the narrow window, a shadow passing in front of the curtain, and he'd crept behind the large oak. The curtain had been parted, just enough for him to peek inside.

He'd told himself he wouldn't linger, would just get a quick glance and be on his way. Satisfy his curiosity about her and leave her alone.

Maggie Dermott had stood in front of her mirror, her blouse removed, both hands cupping large breasts over her functional white bra, massaging them as though they ached.

The sight of her partially disrobed had his body tensing hard, his groin filling quickly.

Her expression held him spellbound.

Pretty, bowed lips parted breathlessly, her eyelids drifted shut, and then she reached behind her to unhook her bra.

When the garment slid away, he'd had his first full view of a woman's mature breasts.

Sure, he'd fondled several classmates, slipped his hands inside their underwear to explore, but he'd never seen anything as beautiful as Maggie Dermott's creamy, rose-tipped breasts.

She'd cupped them in her small hands, just as he imagined he would if he stood behind her, lifting them, her fingers spreading and kneading the pendulous globes.

When she'd plucked the nipples into erect little points, he'd groaned out loud. Their rose hue darkened. The tips drew into tight beads that invited a mouth to sip at them. He imagined drawing on them, rooting into her soft flesh and suckling hard.

When her hands had reached behind her again and slowly slid down the zipper of her denim skirt, he finally admitted to himself he was there for the duration. No possibility of him moving from his vantage outside her window.

Steam rose inside the bathroom. She'd drawn a bath. Foaming bubbles blanketed the surface of the water. Soon she'd sink into the water, and he would leave.

Her skirt slid down her legs. She stood clad only in a demure, pink pair of cotton panties. From the side, her bottom flared, rounded, lush. Perfect.

His cock strained against his zipper, and he reached down to adjust himself, but his hand lingered. He cupped his balls and squeezed, then slid along the erection growing increasingly more insistent as it dragged against his pant leg.

He slid open his belt, unbuttoned the top snap, and scraped down the zipper, intending only to relieve the pressure. Instead he drew his cock outside his pants and wrapped his fingers around his shaft, his gaze never straying from Maggie as she pushed her panties down her legs and stepped out of them. Then she faced the window as she leaned over the bathtub to turn off the water.

The thatch of dark brown hair between her legs was glossy, the curls tight, masking her sex until she opened her legs and stepped over the rim of the tub.

She paused with one foot sinking into the water, the other still on the floor, and reached for the white bar of soap lying on a dish beside the sink.

Her feminine folds parted, giving Danny a glimpse of tightly furled pink labia.

His hand fisted, gliding slowly up and down, drawing blood into his thickening staff. He spit into his other palm and coated his shaft with it, easing his fingers through the moisture.

Lord, she was beautiful. Sleek, pearly skin, rounded thighs and calves, a soft, fleshy bottom beneath a deeply indented waist. Her breasts drew his attention again.

So close now that he could see perspiration glazing the tops of her breasts, his hand tightened, beginning to pump in earnest on his aching cock.

She gathered the soap, a washcloth, and slipped into the water, settling with a visible sigh, laying her head against the rolled rim of the large tub, the tips of her hair dragging in the water.

Her eyes closed and her chest rose, her breasts lifting the bubbles.

He stared for long moments, feeling the urgent heat settling in his balls, knowing it wouldn't be long before he spilled his seed into the dirt.

Her eyes opened and slid to the washcloth. She rolled the soap and cloth inside her hands and then dipped the cloth beneath the water. Her knees rose, parting to fall against each side of the tub, and her hands reached between them.

Her eyes squeezed shut, her pink mouth opened around a gasp, and he knew what she was doing.

The pleasure flushing her cheeks with heightened color was reflected in the pout of her lips and the crease deepening between her eyebrows.

He slowed his hand, wanting to wait and ride the crest with her, to share this intimacy even if she never knew.

Although hidden by the cloud of bubbles, he could tell when she neared the peak. Her neck arched, her knees drew higher. When she came, the water lapped toward the edge of the tub as a muffled but audible moan tightened her lips.

Danny's hips had thrust forward, spearing through his tightly wrapped fingers, desperation making him reckless as he pumped faster, the wet, slapping sounds growing louder until his balls exploded and cum burst from the tip of his cock to stripe the dirt in glistening white. He sagged against the tree, at last closing his eyes.

Immediately a hot wave of shame dampened his pleasure.

God, he was bastard. He'd spied on her, violated her privacy.

With shaking hands, he'd tugged his clothing together and slunk like the snake he was back to his bedroom where he'd jacked off in the dark to the memory of her beautiful, womanly curves every night until he'd finally gone home.

Danny stripped the burning end from his cigarette and pocketed the butt and then quietly entered the house. He undressed in the dark, sitting on the edge of the bed to wrestle off his boots and then standing to strip his belt from its loops and push his pants down his legs.

Naked at last, he tried to ignore the pressure growing between his legs. *A bath? No, a cold shower.*

Danny heard the creak of a floorboard in the hallway outside his bedroom and nearly groaned. He'd been on the edge of arousal, remembering every lurid moment. Now the object of his obsession walked a few feet away.

The sound outside his bedroom cinched tight around his balls. He gave up trying to control the hard-on steadily growing between his legs.

To ease the ache, he spread his legs and fisted his hand around himself, coming in minutes, wanting it over quickly to ease the excitement humming through his veins before he sought his first meeting with the woman whose face and body had owned his lust for over seven years.

2

Danny Tynan was all grown up.

Maggie had noticed that fact right off. She'd hidden in the house like a coward when he arrived that morning, watching him through the curtains as Reggie greeted him with a handshake and a manly slap to his shoulders.

And such broad shoulders they were, too. Something else she'd noticed. He'd been tall as a teenager, all elbows and knobby knees, but anyone looking at him then would easily guess he'd grow into a handsome man.

He'd far exceeded her expectations.

Dark brown hair curled in careless, spiked waves around his head. Thick eyebrows shadowed brown eyes that could melt a woman's heart in a single glance. Those features hadn't changed.

What had changed took her breath away. He turned and stood with his back to her, feet braced apart. She took the opportunity that presented itself, letting her gaze embrace the breadth of his shoulders, the narrow indent of his lean waist, the small, round globes of his buttocks, and thighs that looked sturdy, powerful. . . .

If she'd thought him distracting when he was young, he was lethal to her peace of mind now.

Not that she'd ever acted on her attraction when he'd stayed at the ranch all those years ago. Although she'd entertained lurid fantasies in which she'd played teacher to his youthful sexual education, she'd studiously ignored his adoring glances. Still, she hadn't been able to resist deepening their connection, appealing to a young man's endless appetite. . . .

For food, that is. She'd always loved to bake. Used it when she needed to work out her problems, a kind of "kitchen" therapy that soothed her restlessness when she hammered a slab of steak or kneaded a loaf of bread.

And she'd needed that release during the years of her marriage to Douglas. For, while her husband had been ideal in many ways, he'd left her unfulfilled in two.

The man had never given her an orgasm, never realized the need to provide her passion. He'd provided her a roof, a purpose, given her a home to transform into her own haven.

Though not a handsome man, he'd still managed to impress her when he began to court her. Promising her comfort, protection—family. Something she'd craved since she'd been left alone in the world.

And although he'd tried to fulfill the promise of giving her family, that was another hole he'd left in her life. He'd been sterile. When they'd discovered the fact, he no longer thought it necessary to use her body. What was the point?

When Danny Tynan came to the ranch, she'd met a good-looking boy about to be a man, and a very sexual creature if the state of his bedding was any indication.

Perhaps the hormones raging in his young body had affected her, for she began to feel those stirrings again. The ones her husband's neglect had buried. She'd felt shame for her feelings, for the yearnings that tempted her to leave open a button or two at the top of her blouse to tempt him to peer inside her shirt, to wear shorter shorts to feel his glance rake the length of them.

That was as far as she'd allowed it to go because she hadn't trusted herself to do the right thing.

Now he was back. More of a temptation than ever. But it was much too late for her.

She'd seen his résumé come in on the fax machine, not believing she was reading the name at the top of the form. She'd hidden it, carrying it around all day, debating whether to show it to Reggie.

They'd needed someone like him. She remembered how Douglas had spoken of the young man, about his natural talent with horses, his gentleness when he trained them, how he'd settled a saddle on a particularly fractious stallion inside a day and had him quivering but quiescent as he'd slowly added weight to the young horse's back.

In the end, it hadn't been Danny's talent that had convinced her to give the application to Reggie. She'd needed Danny to come. To see him and to discover that he wasn't as handsome as she remembered and couldn't have been anything more than the sexual fixation of a very frustrated woman. Seeing him again should dull the luster of her memories.

And she'd try anything to dull the wild and inappropriate attraction she'd felt for the boy.

Reggie had taken one look at the crumpled paper she'd shoved at him, and his bushy eyebrows rose high. "Danny Tynan," he'd said quietly. "Seems pretty eager. Says he's free and clear to start right away." His gaze rose from the paper and gave her a searching look. "We've needed some new blood around here."

Maggie shrugged, not wanting to make the decision that would place temptation squarely in her path. "It's up to you," she said, forcing a bright, unconcerned smile.

She'd turned on her heels and fled the office they shared.

When Reggie had mentioned later that day that Danny would be arriving in the morning, she'd given him another vague smile, knowing the wily old man saw right through her.

After a sleepless night filled with second and third thoughts about the wisdom of hiring Danny, and a firm resolution not to let his presence change a single thing, Maggie had played the coward. She'd avoided him all day, breathed a sigh of relief when he hadn't shown up at suppertime, and then retreated to her room right after it to make sure their paths didn't cross.

The sound of his shower starting down the hall quieted her nerves for the first time that long day.

For all the stern talking she'd done with herself, she'd never worked up the courage to confront herself over why she'd decided to let him sleep under her own roof again.

Not once had she considered putting him in the bunkhouse. She'd given him his old room, having always thought of it that way—as his.

Reggie had given her a strange look when she'd told him but held his tongue. Reggie knew how things had been between Douglas and her even before her husband had fallen ill. After Douglas had been diagnosed, their relationship had grown even more remote.

Maybe Reggie didn't question her, because he thought her sexless anyway.

Or maybe he was more compassionate than that.

Even if she wouldn't act on her desires, the thought of Danny sleeping under the same roof filled her with more excitement, more hope than she'd felt stirring inside herself for years.

She wasn't going to feel guilty about it. Wasn't going to feel ashamed. It was time to stop hiding.

First, she needed to make some pies. Something to help her soothe her breathless anticipation and help her sleep.

Flinging on a night robe, she opened her bedroom door to head to the kitchen and slammed into a solid wall of muscle.

Hands reached out to steady her, settling at the tops of her hips. She froze with her arms locked at her sides, gazing up into the brown-eyed gaze that had haunted her for so long.

Only thin layers of cotton separated her chest from his. Her nipples sprouted instantly. "I'm sorry," she said, tilting her head to look fully into his face. "I didn't see you."

Although the hallway was shadowed, she did see the way his lips twisted and heard the swiftly indrawn breath that pressed his chest harder against hers.

"Didn't mean to startle you," he said, his voice sounding gruff.

She shivered at the low timbre of his voice. "I thought you were asleep," she said quickly, trying not to take too deep a breath to keep her nipples from poking against his chest. Though she was only gently pressed against him now, the sensation was wreaking havoc with her mind.

He cleared his throat. "I got hungry."

Her mouth suddenly went dry. She swallowed hard. "I can make you a sandwich. From leftovers," she said, trying to get her tongue and her mind to work together.

However, the large hands bracketing her hips made her legs weak and her tongue stick to the top of her mouth.

"You don't have to. I know where the kitchen is. My own

damn fault I missed dinner." His fingers tightened, and he gave his head a slight shake. "Pardon me."

"For what?" she asked dumbly.

"Cussin'."

"I don't mind; I'm surrounded by men. I know how you talk," she said softly, charmed by his attempt to mind his manners and beginning to grow warm inside his embrace. "You can let me go now. I won't fall."

His breath hitched, and his hands dropped as if they'd been burned.

Instantly she missed the heat of his fingers, the strength in his hands, but she turned, tucking her head down to hide her expression as she pursed her lips and blew a silent whistle.

Danny followed her, keeping just a step behind her all the way into the kitchen.

With a tall, handsome man trailing her through her home, she'd never felt so aware of herself, of the sway of her hips, of her shorter height, or of her femininity.

When she reached the kitchen, breathless and flustered, she turned on the lights and then wished she hadn't been so quick. She wore a white cotton gown with a thin white robe over it. He might see something if the cloth pulled too close to her body or her figure was silhouetted in the light.

As soon as the thought flitted through her mind, another followed closely: would he like what he saw?

She stopped hunching her shoulders—which was hiding the sharp points of her nipples—and concentrated instead on pulling out slices of freshly baked ham and bread and the rest of the "fixings" a young man might appreciate.

He didn't have to know she deliberately displayed herself. It would be her wicked little secret. One to savor in the darkness when she returned to her lonely bed.

In the meantime, she watched him from the corners of her eyes, catching his glance darting toward her bare legs and then rising higher, snagging on her chest as she stood on tiptoe to reach for glasses from the cupboard.

"Let me," he said quietly, reaching over her shoulder into the high second shelf.

His body leaned against her back, a thickly muscled arm entering her sight as he stretched past her to take down two glasses.

He'd never know how her body trembled as he pressed closer and his rich, masculine scent poured over her.

"Got it," he whispered.

Startled, her glance swung to his.

Or maybe he did know.

Standing so close, the glare of overhead lights illuminated his features, revealing the heat flaring in his deep brown eyes.

A breathy gasp escaped her lips.

Danny blinked and drew away, setting the glasses on the countertop.

Maggie turned and gripped the edge of the counter behind her and watched as he walked stiffly toward the table and sat. He winced, widened his legs under the table, and then rested his forearms on the edge as he clasped his hands together.

He didn't look up. Seemed to studiously avoid looking her way.

Maggie dragged in a deep breath, shaking her head to clear it of the luscious thoughts skittering through her mind.

Pushing away from the counter, she gathered what she needed, made two sandwiches, and portioned out a generous helping of her homemade potato salad. Then she walked over to him, standing beside him to set the plate on the table. "What would you like to drink?"

His head stayed down, color rimming the top of his ear. "Whatever's handy," he muttered.

"Iced tea? Milk?" she said breathlessly.

"Milk, I guess."

She walked away, opened the refrigerator, and then bent to reach inside and pick up the carton. Before she straightened, she cast a glance toward him to find his head turning sharply away.

Dear Lord. Did he find her attractive? After all this time?

With her hair mussed, no makeup, and wearing old cotton nightclothes?

The sight of him, dressed in T-shirt and jeans, his feet bare, was too delicious for her peace of mind. Her hands trembled as she poured milk into the two glasses and carried them to the table. She took a seat opposite him, keeping her gaze on his plate.

She pushed a strand of hair behind her ear and swallowed. "You aren't eating."

He cleared his throat again. "I'm sorry for your loss."

She lifted her head and stared, not understanding. A moment passed as his steady stare held hers before his words registered.

Douglas. He was talking about Doug. "Thank you. He's been gone a while. I've gotten used to it."

That Doug's passing had been a relief at the end, for them both, was a guilty secret she held close to her heart.

His fingers curled on the table beside his plate. "You shouldn't have put me up here."

"You mean in the house?" At his slow nod, she added, "Why?"

"Pretty woman like you. People might talk."

Truly surprised, she blurted, "But I'm older than you."

His eyebrows rose. "Whatever," he muttered.

She took a deep breath and looked around the kitchen, trying not to read too much into his intense expression, trying harder to ignore the excitement heating her body inside and out. "You think I'm pretty?" Dear God, had she really blurted that out?

His snort drew her back. Fascinated, she watched as he deliberately picked up one of the sandwiches and began to eat, holding her gaze all the while as though daring her to comment on what he didn't have to say.

Emboldened by his words, she searched through her mind for the right way to ask him to explain. "I suppose I didn't consider the fact you're a grown man now. Living with any woman in such close proximity . . ." Because she knew she was babbling, she clamped her lips shut.

He swallowed the bite and licked his lips. "Bullshit."

He'd said it so softly she couldn't say she was exactly shocked. His adamancy spurred her rising excitement. "Beg your pardon?"

"Not just any woman. *You.*"

She glanced away as her heartbeats quickened inside her chest. The conversation was quickly becoming more intimate than she thought she could handle, given the arousal slowly building inside her. "Would you be more comfortable in the bunkhouse?"

"Is that what you want?"

Again, his soft-spoken but bluntly stated words cut straight through her.

A boldness she didn't know she possessed told her that if she ever wanted to explore the attraction that sparked between them, now was the time for a little honesty.

Knowing she was taking a step past the point of no return, she closed her eyes and drew a deep, fortifying breath. Then, meeting his gaze, she replied, "No. I don't want you to leave."

3

Danny took another bite, not the least bit hungry but wanting time to think about how to respond. He didn't want to come off sounding desperate, but he wanted her to know he was interested—keenly so.

The feel of her soft, pillowy breasts snuggled up against his chest in the hallway had made him hard in the space of a heartbeat.

As she'd fluttered nervously around the kitchen, he'd watched her, trying not to blatantly stare but looking close enough to see if he was reading the signs right.

He didn't want to make a misstep. Didn't want her shying away, or, worse, becoming embarrassed by him and his horny self.

But having her sitting across the table from him in her thin nightgown, knowing she'd pulled herself straight from her bed, still looking warm and mussed because she couldn't sleep, gave him hope that maybe she shared a little of the attraction that raged through his body.

Perhaps he'd been a little too eager, pressing against her as he'd taken down the glasses, but he couldn't regret it. She'd trembled against him, grown breathless, confirming the arousal that had spiked her nipples against his chest when she'd barreled into him.

Maggie Dermott wanted him. Looked as though she was dying to be fucked—by him.

He'd give a limb for the chance to be with her, to love her all the ways he'd dreamed of loving her for so long.

No way would he blow it. He'd go slow, love her like she deserved. Turn her inside out with all the wicked things he'd do. Make it impossible for her ever to let him go.

First, he needed to convince her he was serious. The crazy woman thought she was too damn old for him.

"Just seems a little strange," he said slowly, "me being here. Only man in the house."

She licked her lips. "I thought you might like your old room."

"I do. A bed's softer than a cot."

A small, tight smile tipped up the corners of her mouth. "It'll be nice having the company."

A flush of anger had him spearing her with a glance. He wasn't going to let her play polite games. Not after she'd managed to get him good and aroused. "Is there anything else you want, Maggie?"

Her eyes widened. Her lips pressed together for a moment. Then she gave him a direct look, one that didn't slide away into any pretense. "Would"—she paused to lick her lips—"would you be totally shocked if I said I want you?"

Danny froze. How was a man supposed to respond when

he'd just been handed heaven on a platter? Deep, visceral satisfaction thrummed inside him, filling his loins with heat.

Her mouth opened around a loud gasp. "I can't believe I just said that. Forget it," she said hastily, her eyes blinking against the welling moisture.

Danny set the last of the sandwich on the plate and reached across the table to clasp her wrist with his fingers. "I'm finished here. Let's go," he said and then bit back a curse at his brash words. Could he sound more like an eager puppy?

She tugged her hand, trying to escape him. Her breaths huffed out with a ragged edge. "I shouldn't have said that."

"Why, if it's what you feel?"

Her brows arched over her lustrous brown eyes. "I feel foolish."

"You don't look it. Not to me."

"But it's wrong for me even to consider it. You and me? I'm too old for you."

Danny couldn't help the edge of irritation that crept into his voice. "You sound as if you're ready for a walker."

"I knew you when you were still in high school." Her expression grew more earnest as she argued. But who was she trying to convince?

"I graduated," he said flatly. "I'm old enough to vote, to smoke, to fuck any woman I want and not send her to jail."

Her nose wrinkled. "That was a little crude."

"That's how I feel. Crude. Raw. A pretty lady just said she wants me."

Her gaze slid away, and her other hand lifted to close the space where her night robe gaped open. "I wish you hadn't said that. I wish you'd tell me you were flattered but maybe it's not such a great idea."

Danny would never understand a woman's mind. She wanted

him. Why not just stop at that? But he knew enough to let her talk. "If you told me the truth, why would you want me to turn you down?"

Her shoulders lifted in a small shrug. "Because I'm afraid."

"Of me?" he asked, truly surprised.

"Of disappointing you."

"Not possible," he muttered.

"I'm not . . . young." Her gaze dropped lower. "My body shows its years."

"Your body felt just fine to me a few minutes ago."

Her eyes closed briefly and then at last opened to meet his gaze. "I'll want the lights off," she whispered.

Danny held himself still, wanting to savor her surrender. He'd been with her less than half an hour, and he couldn't believe things had moved this fast.

She was likely just as shocked. If he gave her any time, any space to reconsider, she might backpedal fast.

Still, he found himself slowly shaking his head. "I'll want them on. I wanna see you."

Her brows drew together in a slight frown.

Was he pushing her too far when he ought to be damned grateful she'd given him that first inch?

Maggie's cheeks billowed as she blew out a deep breath. "I'm not very good."

A smile tugged at the corners of his lips. Her hesitation didn't have a thing to do with whether or not she wanted him bad enough. She was worried about what he'd think.

"Maggie," he said softly, "I'm very, very good."

She glared, and her eyebrows drew together in a tiny frown. "That's supposed to make me feel better?"

He shook his head and pulled her hand toward him. "Just the truth. I'm not letting you change your mind."

Her shoulders straightened. "*If* we do this, it's just this once. Just to get past it."

His grin widened. "Think you can get me out of your system?"

"*And* this stays between us," she said, her glare intensifying. "No one else can know."

"You ashamed of wanting me?"

The way her gaze veered off again said plainly that she was. "I live here. People knew me before, when Doug was still here. I don't want them looking at me different."

Danny remained silent for a moment, not wanting commit to a promise he didn't want to keep, but, in the end, he blew out a deep breath. Maggie wasn't going to budge on this one. "Then it'll be our secret. You finished laying down rules?"

"I guess."

He stood, pulling her up with him, and then turned, switching hands behind him as he led her out the door.

He didn't bother keeping his steps short. Liked hearing her feet skip to keep up as he strode straight down the long hallway to her bedroom.

"Not here," she said breathlessly behind him. "Your room. Please?"

Danny ignored the small pain that sliced through his chest and passed up her door on the way to his own.

Once inside, he turned, flicked on the light switch, and leaned his back against the door.

Her arms crossed at her waist. "Well?"

Feeling a little ornery, he reasoned she deserved to feel some discomfort after everything she'd put him through. "A man likes to watch a woman take off her clothes."

She shook her head, defiance glowing in her brown eyes. "I can't."

"Just the robe, then. Slide it off."

"What about you?"

"After you, sweetheart."

She swallowed hard, opened the tie of her robe, and shrugged it off, letting it pool on the floor behind her. Then her gaze returned to him, one fine brow arching.

Danny leaned away from the door and stripped off his T-shirt, balling it in his fist to toss toward the bathroom door.

He didn't bother to wait for her to balk at removing another piece of clothing and flicked open the button at the top of his jeans. The scrape of the zipper sounded overloud in the silence of the room.

Once accomplished, he peeled down his jeans and straightened, standing nude in front of her for the first time.

The stunned expression on her face tightened his whole body to stone. His dick jerked as her gaze landed on it. Danny held himself still, except for his throbbing cock, waiting while she looked her fill.

Her eyes widened, her pink lips parted on a quiet gasp. "This is wrong in so many ways," she whispered, but her hands gathered the fabric around her thighs and pulled up her cotton nightgown, baring her body except for a narrow pair of bikini panties.

Danny's gaze devoured her full breasts, swept down her softly rounded tummy and clung to the scrap of fabric still shielding her sex. "Take it off," he growled.

Her fingers shook as she hooked her thumbs along the sides of her panties and slowly rolled them down. When she stepped out of them, she lifted her face, looking more than a little anxious.

"You're beautiful, Maggie Dermott," he said, his voice sounding rough to his own ears.

They stood for the longest time, both naked, both staring. Danny wanted to take the first step forward but needed a little time to plan the best approach to give her the maximum pleasure.

Only, he couldn't think. Couldn't breathe.

She was so damned beautiful. Round swells, deep troughs; her body was a little heavier than he remembered, but the curves only accentuated her femininity.

An urgent throb entered his groin, impossible to ignore. He stepped toward her, slowly lifted a hand, and curved it around her cheek. Then, holding her gaze, he leaned down to capture her lips.

How right it felt, sharing their first kiss without a scrap of clothing between them. He lapped at her lips, drinking in her nervous little pants before stroking the tip of his tongue inside to touch hers. Their tongues pressed together and then slid alongside each other, stroking slowly in and out.

He lifted his free hand and gently cupped one soft breast and nearly groaned into her mouth. Softer than anything he'd ever felt, the flesh beneath his palm was warm and quivering with her shortened breaths.

The tip of her nipple dragged across his palm, and urgency gripped him harder. He had to have it in his mouth. Needed to taste her now.

He lifted his head, spearing her with a glance that told her not to bother complaining, and then knelt on one knee in front of her.

Everything that followed was pure instinct, pure pleasure.

He pressed a kiss between her breasts and nuzzled the sides of both with his cheeks. Then he began to press wet, open-mouthed kisses against them, one at a time, as he held both in his hands and gently massaged.

The soft, clean scent of her, baby powder and plain soap, a dab of something floral between her breasts, the ripening scent of her moist sex . . .

God, he couldn't get enough.

Her hands landed softly on the tops of his shoulders and fluttered as though she wasn't sure where to put them.

He paused, reached up to grab them, and lifted them to his head, his palms flattening against the back of her hands to guide her fingers through his hair. "Don't be afraid to touch me. You can't hurt me. Pull, if you like. Scratch if you feel the need."

Her lips curved slowly, and she tugged on his hair.

His eyes half closed, and his mouth opened around a groan. Then he leaned forward again to finally root at her breast the way he'd always imagined.

She swayed toward him, murmuring something so low he couldn't make it out, but the soft, desperate edge to her voice burned him, and he opened his jaws wide to suck as much of her rounded breast as he could take into his mouth.

He suckled hard, laving the tip with his tongue inside his mouth, over and over. When her hands tugged his hair to move him to the other, he let her guide him, loving the second breast like he had the first until her knees buckled, and he rose swiftly to scoop her up into his arms and carry her to the bed.

He crawled onto the mattress without letting her go, taking her to the middle and laying her down before crawling right on top of her.

Lying beneath him, staring up at him, her face was flushed, her lips plump and pink. Her eyelids dipped as though her arousal was already in full bloom.

He bent to press a quick kiss to her lips. "I'll try to go slow," he said quietly, "but I'm not sure I can hold back much longer."

"Then don't," she whispered. "I'm dying to feel you inside

me." Her legs opened beneath him, her knees rising to frame the sides of his hips.

Danny rose on one elbow and leaned to the side, trailing a hand slowly down her belly before spearing through her curls and sliding his fingers into the moisture gathered between her folds.

Her pussy clasped around his fingers, making sexy, juicy little pulses that had his dick jerking in anticipation. He pulled his fingers away, spread the moisture over the sensitive cap of his cock, and guided himself to her opening.

Settling directly over her again, he prodded her entrance, watching as her eyes closed and her mouth opened around a breathless moan. He stroked the tip slowly in and out, drawing more liquid from her body until he thought her passage lubricated and pliant enough to take more of him.

Then, gathering his knees under him, he ground his teeth together and thrust his cock, slowly, all the way inside.

Her hips lifted upward, taking him that much deeper.

He glided straight into smooth, creamy silk. He sucked in a deep breath, pausing at the end, letting out a painful groan. Then he began to move, pushing and pulling his cock through honey-coated walls that felt like a gentle, wet fist closing around him.

Her head turned away, her eyes still closed, and she lifted her hands to cup the corners of his shoulders.

Something wasn't right. She was too quiet, lying too still beneath him. He wasn't getting it. Wasn't bringing her along.

He leaned away, making just enough space to slide a hand down her belly, his fingers searching for the nubbin at the top of her sex.

With her labia stretched around his cock, he found the little bump but wasn't satisfied it was engorged enough. His thumb pushed up the hood protecting it, and he began to swirl a finger across the top—gauging her comfort with the contact of his calloused finger by the little jerks of her hips—until she settled and began to rock against him.

Then, with his finger gliding over the burgeoning knot, he deepened his thrusts.

Her teeth clamped down on her upper lip, and her head turned deeper into the coverlet beneath her.

"It's all right, Maggie. Make some noise, baby," he began to croon. "Let me know when I get it right. I'm here. I won't let you go. Won't stop until you scream for me."

Her head shook, and her face crumpled. Moisture gathered at the seams of her tightly closed eyes.

"Baby, come with me," he whispered.

At last, he felt a gush of hot liquid seep around his cock, engulfing him in the warm honey spilling from her depths.

Her mouth opened, a small, shattered cry tearing from her. Her back arched, her fingernails dug deep into his skin.

Danny gritted his teeth, kept his motions even, unchanging, so he wouldn't stall her orgasm, waiting while her body trembled and arched and her pussy clasped around him in gentle convulsions.

When her body relaxed beneath him, he pulled away his hand and lay down on top of her. He framed her face with his palms, waiting until she slowly opened her eyes.

When her sleepy brown gaze finally met his, he said, "Tell me that's not the first time you ever had an orgasm with a man."

4

_____

Maggie's eyes widened.

As if she'd just been dashed with cold water, the warm, lazy lassitude she'd experienced was gone in an instant.

What had she just done? How could she have abandoned every bit of common sense and propriety on which she'd prided herself and invited herself into this *cowboy's* bed?

She inserted her hands between their bodies and shoved. "Get off me."

His heavy body didn't budge.

Still pinned beneath him, his cock locked inside her, she squirmed as panic began to consume her.

How had he guessed he'd been her first? What business was it of his? If she allowed him to question her, to wheedle the truth from her, she felt as though she'd betray Douglas. And wasn't she just as much at fault?

"Get off me," she repeated, continuing to push.

"Maggie," he began and then encircled her wrists and pushed her hands up to rest on either side of her head.

She continued to wriggle beneath him, planting her feet in the mattress to get more leverage to buck him off, but he rolled his hips from one side to the other, capturing her legs one at a time beneath his.

When she was completely blanketed, unable to move, growing breathless with her fruitless struggles, only then did she fall still. "Why are you doing this?" she gritted out, unable to meet his steady gaze.

"I asked you a question."

"One I'm not willing to answer. It's none of your business."

"Probably not, but I think you need to let it out."

"Who made you Dr. Phil?"

His lips twisted into a wry smile. Yet his eyes darkened, a sadness entering his expression that was just too hard for her to face.

She closed her eyes. "This . . . with you . . . it's just . . ."

"Just what? Just fucking?"

She winced, opened her eyes, and turned her head aside to avoid his gaze. Fucking him hadn't felt as intimate as this conversation. "Yes. That's all it can be. You don't have any right to ask about my life with my husband."

"He'd dead, Maggie."

"It's not fair to him. I won't speak badly of him. He was a good man."

"But maybe not such a good husband?"

"Just because he never—"

"He didn't care enough to make sure you were happy."

"I wasn't . . . unhappy." She spoke the lie, knowing her hesitation gave away her doubts.

Danny sighed so deeply she felt the ragged exhalation shudder against her chest. "Tell me."

Maggie slowly turned her head, tears welling at the concern etched in his tight features. Why did he care? His cock filled her, hard and pulsing. Why wasn't he just taking what she offered?

"Maggie . . ."

The insistence in his voice, the implacable weight pinning her to the bed, told her he wasn't moving until she shared.

"Why can't you leave it alone? It's over. *Years* over."

He bent and placed a soft kiss beside her mouth and then moved back again. "I'm still waiting.

And though she'd never shared her disappointments with another living soul, suddenly words were spilling from her lips. "Damn you, I don't want to talk about this," she whispered. Her fingers curled, her nails biting into her palms. "He was older than me. A little set in his ways. He didn't mind I didn't know a gelding from a stallion, wasn't raised on a ranch, and wouldn't be any help there. All he wanted was someone to keep his home clean and provide meals for the men." She blew out a breath. "You know, this might be easier if I could actually breathe."

"For some ranchers, that's plenty," he said quietly, completely ignoring her complaint. However, he did rise on his elbows, lifting a little weight from her chest.

"Thank you," she replied with a touch of sarcasm. "But I always felt like I was getting the better half of the bargain. He worked so hard." She halted again, swallowing because the rest was going to be hard.

Danny's palm cupped her cheek, and his thumb swept her lower lip once. "He worked morning to night? Not much time for the two of you to be alone?"

She nodded, glad he understood, because she didn't think she explained herself very well. Talking was hard when she found herself lying beneath a handsome, virile male. "We tried

117

at first. We both wanted children. When it didn't happen, I had to push him to come to the doctor with me. That's when we discovered he couldn't get me pregnant. I think he felt . . ."

"Less like a man?" he asked softly.

She nodded again, keeping her expression set despite the jagged pain shooting through her chest. "We just stopped," she said, her voice tightening. "I mean, what was the point?"

His eyes gleamed with compassion—so much of it she found herself blinking away tears.

"The point should have been that you two needed each other."

She gave him a brittle smile. "Well, it didn't work that way for us. I guess there just wasn't enough love to work through it. And then he got sick." She pressed her lips together and turned away. "Are we done?" she asked dully.

His hand smoothed over her hair, and he pressed a kiss to her forehead. "Well, now I know. I won't ever make you go there again."

Now that she'd gotten it out, the tension inside her did relax. With his hand still smoothing over her hair, she closed her eyes and pushed against his hand, needing the comfort of his touch.

Gradually she grew more intensely aware of the heaviness pressing down on her body, the unyielding hardness filling her. Her breaths deepened, and a small echo of a tremor rippled along her channel.

"Maggie . . . ?"

"Please," she whispered.

He murmured something low and deliciously obscene and then slowly flexed his hips, tunneling into her.

Liquid seeped from inside her, easing the hot friction between his cock and her inner walls. "Let me move," she said, straining her hips against him.

"I can't hold back," he ground out.

"Don't want you to."

"I wanted to give you pleasure."

"Later. Let me see yours."

His features tightened; rich color flooded his cheeks. "You can't know how good this feels. Me inside you. *Jesus!*"

He released her hands and set his on the mattress, rising above her. A knee nudged between hers, and she opened eagerly, lifting her legs to tilt her sex and take him deeper.

His cock withdrew and slid back inside. They both groaned as he filled her, thrusting through her wet heat. He gathered his knees beneath him and began to stroke in earnest.

Unbelievably to her, desire rekindled, sharp and insistent. Maggie slid her arms around his back and smoothed over tense muscle, tracing the deep indentation of his spine and flowing downward to his hard, round buttocks.

She stared as passion tightened his whole body, transforming him from the considerate lover, who'd gently gifted her with her first orgasm, into a feral male.

His jaw flexed, his nostrils flared, his gaze held hers, and then he jerked upward, rising higher on his arms and glancing down between their bodies.

Her glance followed, skimming his rippling chest and arms, trailing down the muscles that bunched along his deeply tanned abdomen, giving her a view of a six-pack she'd seen only in magazine ads.

But that wasn't what he wanted her to see.

Trailing lower, her gaze caught on the sight of his thick cock gliding in and out of her body—slick, satiny, coated in smears of white cream. *Hers.*

A cry forced its way through her tight throat. Her arousal spiked hard, but she couldn't tear away her gaze, feeling every inch of him cramming inside, dragging outward and then tunneling deep again and again.

She squeezed her inner muscles around him, watching him pause to savor her clasp. He grunted as he shoved back inside past her pale resistance. Then he began to circle his hips, screwing himself in and out.

Maggie's belly began to tremble; her breaths gusted in thin, wispy moans. She let go of his shoulders and scraped her fingers down his chest, tugging at his hair, sliding in his perspiration, reaching lower until she raked her fingers through the curls at the base of his cock.

Her fingers encircled him, attempting to ring him but coming up short. Lord, she didn't know how they ever fit. But the girth straining beneath her fingers as he continued to thrust explained the fullness, the divine pressure he exerted against her passage.

She lifted her gaze to find him staring.

"Want more?" he asked. "Wanna come again?"

With his voice tight, his body even more so, she didn't know how he held it together, how he didn't explode as he stroked inside her.

She nodded, trusting he knew exactly how to get her off. After all, he'd already accomplished the miracle once.

He pulled out, placing both hands on his thighs, and dragged deep breaths into his lungs. "Turn over."

God, he'd be behind her. Get an eyeful of her big butt. She began to rethink.

"No, you don't," he said tightly. "I'm in pain here. I'm not letting you change your mind."

A smile tugged at her lips. Danny might be her junior, but he sure liked being in charge.

She liked it, too. So, taking a deep breath, she slid her legs to one side of his and rolled to her belly, coming up on her hands and knees.

"Sweet Jesus," he murmured, his hands smoothing over her ass.

"Not another word," she warned. "I might still change my mind."

"You think I don't like this view?"

She snorted and glanced back to gauge his expression. From the way his lips pursed, he didn't seem to mind. A dangerous gleam shone in his eyes. "Thought we were going to get busy," she huffed.

"I am. I will. Just let me enjoy this for a minute, huh?"

She issued a strained laugh and tried not to fall on her face when he began to firmly massage her bottom, lifting her buttocks and rolling them as his hands squeezed harder around her flesh.

Something began to happen as she watched him staring at her. Some of the insecurities she'd carried for a long, long time melted away. She arched her back, determined to take as much enjoyment and provide as much of a tease as she had the nerve to deliver.

Her bottom rose higher, and she spread her thighs wider on the windowpane comforter.

His gaze narrowed, aimed right between her legs.

She braced her weight on one hand and reached beneath her, slipping her fingers between her folds to swirl.

Danny's fingers dug so deep she knew he'd leave bruises on her tender skin, but she didn't care. The look on his face was compensation enough for the sexy marks.

Suddenly he bent low to slide hot kisses over her cool skin.

Her fingers circled faster. Her forefinger dipped inside her channel and came out soaked in her excitement. She used the moisture to skim lightly over her swelling clitoris.

His mouth glided toward the center of her buttocks, and her breath hitched when his tongue traced the crease, pausing to lap at her forbidden entrance, an action she would never have conceived of as being pleasurable, but a tremor shook her body, and her breath rasped.

She didn't bother trying to complain for modesty's sake—it felt too damn good.

His tongue circled again and then lifted from her. "Liked that, did you?" he asked, his tone laced with lazy amusement.

"Loved it," she softly croaked.

"Trust me?"

A loaded question, from her perspective. "What do you want to do?"

"I'd spoil the surprise." His mild rebuke was tinged with more humor.

Her lips pressed together, and she faced forward, lowering her head to rest against the bedding. "Am I going to be able to look you in the eye tomorrow?"

"Not without blushing."

"Oh, Lord," she muttered, "you've already assured that."

"That would just be closing the gate after the cow came home."

"What the hell does that mean, anyway?" she asked, her shoulders shaking.

"Not a clue."

"So long as it didn't come to mind while you were looking . . . where you're looking."

Low, masculine laughter filled the room. A hand lifted and then landed on her backside, startling her.

"Just making sure I had your attention."

"You've had it since you were—" She cut off the retort before she finished it, realizing the rest would have been too revealing.

"A boy?" His voice rose in mock surprise. "Maggie Dermott, were you lusting after me when I was still in high school?"

"Of course not," she said a little too quickly.

Another light swat, and he growled, "The feeling was mutual, ma'am."

"Oh, shut up. I'm ashamed of the fact."

"Why? It was a natural thing. You had the good sense not to act on it."

Her mind raced. Sure, she'd had good sense. She'd left buttons open on her blouse. Worn shorts so brief a slight bend would have shown the cheeks of her ass.

And she'd left her bathroom curtains open.

"I was married. I had no right to even think about it—and you were too damn young."

"Not so damn young I didn't dream about you at night." His breaths left a hot, humid trail over her bottom again. "I lay in this bed, naked as the day I was born, wishing you'd slip down the hall and peek inside. Know what you would have seen?"

"I washed your sheets. I have an idea."

His tongue flicked out and traced one side of her labia and then the other. "I watched you," he whispered against her sex; then he thrust his tongue inside her.

She jerked against him, her finger toggling fast on her clit. Her belly tightened as arousal coiled like a spring deep inside her.

His mouth drew on her lips, sucking on them while he continued to spear her with his tongue. Then his hand closed around her finger and drew it down.

He sucked her finger into his mouth, licking it clean and then dropping it. "No cheating."

Then he straightened behind her, his hands reaching for the tops of her hips. His cock prodded between her folds, nudging, circling until he was centered on her entrance.

When he thrust inside, she balled her fists in the coverlet and moaned. She'd never felt anything so exquisitely erotic in her life—his thick cock shoving past her swollen inner tissues, thrusting in and out, inching forward as he lifted her bottom toward him to angle deeper.

She rolled her face to the side. "What did you mean, you watched me?"

He stroked harder inside her, shoving all the way in. "Through your bathroom window," he rasped. "I watched you pleasure yourself."

Oh, God! The night Douglas had gone to San Antonio. The one night she'd given in to her fantasy. She'd left the drapes parted, just a few inches, never expecting he would notice.

Just the thought that he might had been enough to rocket her toward ecstasy. A sob broke free, and she planted her face in the bedding, even as his sure, straight strokes tunneled deep inside her body, capturing the arousal coiling tighter inside her.

"I did it on purpose," she whispered. "I wanted you to watch. I was so damn desperate for it. Too far gone to think about consequences. I never really thought you'd see. But it didn't matter."

"When you came, were you thinking about me?" he asked, not missing a stroke.

"Yes!"

His hips gathered strength, and suddenly his slow, juicy glides gained speed, each one ending on a jarring stroke that tapped the mouth of her womb.

Her body began to tremble, and she eased apart her knees a little farther, let her back sink deeper, and tilted her ass higher to receive the full force of his thrusts.

Danny's hands pushed and pulled her hips, bringing her in when he hammered forward, pushing her away when he withdrew.

So much moisture seeped from inside her soon the room was filled with wet, slurping sounds, so decadent, so raw they only added to the excitement unfurling inside her.

Danny's strokes grew in power, and Maggie's chest rubbed up and down the coverlet, her nipples scraping the cotton until she felt as though every inch of her body was being seduced toward an orgasm.

Sure she wouldn't last a second longer, she gave a thin scream when a finger traced between her buttocks and then nudged against her asshole.

When the tip slipped inside, she shoved off the mattress and began to slam backward to meet his thrusts.

He tunneled deeper, the tender tissues squeezing tight around his finger, burning, convulsing as a strong, writhing ripple worked its way down her vagina.

"That's it, baby," he said, his voice sounding strained and hoarse. "Go with it. *Fuck!*"

His finger pumped inside her as his hips jackhammered into her pussy.

A high, keening cry tore from her, and Maggie was sure the top of her head had exploded. Light dimmed around her, narrowing to a tunnel. The prickling darkness lifted goose bumps all over her body and crackled in her ears.

Molten liquid jetted deep inside her body, and then she was falling, her body shuddering so hard she couldn't hold herself up.

His finger pulled free, but he followed her down, continuing to rut against her, slowing gradually until he, too, shook against her, jerking as the last emanations bathed her channel.

He laid on top of her, stretching slowly to cover her, running his hands up her arms and then threading his fingers through hers. His lips planted kisses against her shoulder and then her cheek, and she turned as far back as she could to capture his lips in a kiss.

When their breaths began to even out, he drew away and rested his head on the bed beside her. "Trust me now?"

5

All morning long, Maggie worked steadily, trying to keep her focus on her chores, while inside she was a bundle of conflicting emotions.

Last night had happened so fast she hadn't had time to think. She'd acted instinctively on the arousal he inspired in her, and she'd gone with those feelings to places she'd never imagined— into sinful pleasures that even now she had to really work hard to feel ashamed about.

She was a fallen woman. A hussy. Her body warmed at the thought. Shouldn't she be appalled with herself?

Instead she felt liberated, lighter at heart. Having always believed herself a sensible person, she'd been delighted to discover she could also be terribly, wonderfully slutty.

She'd fucked a younger man. Practically begged him to do it. She'd paraded herself in her nightclothes, rubbed her body against his, and let him know in no uncertain terms that she was available.

She couldn't blame him for taking her up on her offer. Didn't resent his eager acceptance. That he'd turned the tables on her and taken control from her, she couldn't regret.

The man definitely knew what he was about.

However, as happy and as satisfied as she felt the morning after, sadness lingered at the edges of her happy little bubble.

She couldn't let their affair continue. Someone had to act responsibly. It had to be her. Not that she'd acted all that responsibly the night before.

Not once had she paused to ask him to use a condom.

She couldn't blame the lapse on the heat of the moment, nor on her lack of experience using them—she'd wanted his seed. Needed to take the reckless chance that, just maybe, she might conceive. The urge had been overwhelming.

Maggie found flowers on the kitchen counter wrapped in two white plastic bags to conceal them. A dozen red roses she brought automatically to her nose to inhale their sweet fragrance.

The flowers were a lovely gesture that spoke of his pleasure in her, his affection even, but were still a gesture she wasn't sure she felt comfortable with.

Last night had been a revelation, but that was as far as she could allow things to go between them. Pleasure seemed to flow as easily as breath between them whenever they touched, and that scared the hell out of her.

She simply couldn't let him get close enough again to compromise her decision. She needed to set things straight with him right away.

Danny wasn't hard to find. He worked alone in the training corral at the far side of the stable, a buckskin quarter horse circling him on a long rope.

She wiped at the perspiration that dotted her forehead and

upper lip and then admitted it was a futile gesture. Even if it weren't summertime in Texas, she'd be sweating.

Dressed in a straw cowboy hat, jeans, and a dark tee, Danny's lean, muscled body drew her hungry gaze despite her inner warning to keep this light and nonchalant. She'd politely thank him for the roses, remind him of their agreement, and be on her way.

She climbed onto the split-rail fence to watch as he clucked and flicked the end of the coiled rope he held at the horse's flanks to keep him moving.

Danny turned and flashed a quick, easy smile and then slowed the horse, pulling it ever closer as he coiled the rope around his arm.

When the horse finally came to a halt, Danny smoothed his hand over the horse's head and neck, rubbed the side of his nose, and leaned in to whisper his praise before grabbing the bottom of the halter to lead him toward Maggie.

"Mornin'," Danny said softly, his gaze sweeping over her face and then down over her cotton blouse and blue jeans. The heat that flared in his eyes was banked but palpable.

Looking down at him, Maggie drew in a deep breath. "You didn't have to do that."

A single brow rose, and his eyes narrowed. "No, I didn't. And it doesn't come with a price, Maggie. I'm not expecting anything."

She should have felt comforted, but instead warmth filled her cheeks. Ashamed for her ungracious attitude, she added, "I love roses. What female doesn't?"

He nodded, set the coiled rope over the top of a fence post, and turned back to her. "But . . . ?"

"Last night was just that: one night."

He glanced away, his lips tightening. "I'm not gonna say the roses didn't mean something. A man should let a woman know he doesn't take a thing for granted."

"We had a deal."

"I know. But I really hoped you'd change your mind."

When he lifted his gaze to hers again, his expression made her tremble. Need, confusion, heat, even a little anger . . . all those emotions were stamped on his taut features.

"I don't know what you thought this would be. . . ." Her whispered words trailed off because her throat tightened and her eyes began to burn.

Damnit, she wasn't going to cry.

"Last night was special," Danny whispered harshly. "I felt the connection. You can't tell me something didn't happen between us."

"Something did," she admitted. "And you know how incredible it was for me, but I'm not looking for a relationship. And you wouldn't be the man I'd choose if I were."

His chest expanded around a deep, indrawn breath. "Because I'm too young?"

"You have your whole life in front of you."

His angry glance sliced. "That's bullshit. You aren't thinking about me. You're thinking about being embarrassed by being seen with me."

"I'm thinking further ahead than just getting a little more satisfaction tonight."

His head lowered, his expression hidden by the brim of his hat. Then he straightened and placed his hands on the rails on either side of her thighs. "You think I haven't considered everything? Where this might lead? I have plenty to offer you, Maggie. And you're everything I want."

With him standing so close, surrounding her, her body warmed and softened. "You say that now . . ."

He leaned in closer, his eyes narrowing on her face, a muscle flexing hard along the side of his strong jaw. "You think when those little wrinkles beside your eyes deepen, or your body gets a little rounder, that I won't want you? That I'll leave you?"

She shook her head slowly, sadness curving her lips downward. "It would be so much worse because I know you wouldn't. You'd stay because you'd feel obligated, and I had that before. My life wasn't fun. I was lonely as hell."

"Why not give it a chance? See where it goes? I can take it slow. If you think I don't know my mind, give me time to make sure."

"I can't," she said brokenly.

The set of his square jaw softened. "Why, Maggie? I deserve to know why."

She shook her head, glancing beyond his shoulder. "Because I don't want that kind of pain. Can't risk it. What I felt for Doug at the start was nothing like this."

Danny moved closer, and he lifted a hand to cup over hers as she gripped the rails. "It's intense, isn't it? The air crackles when we're together like lightning strikin' close."

"Exactly," she said flatly, pulling her hand from beneath his. "When it ends, that feeling won't just gently fade away."

"Are you in love with me?" he said softly.

"No . . . I don't know," she said, hearing the pain and confusion feather the edge of her voice. "I'm plenty in lust with you, though. It's damn confusing. I know what I don't need, and you're it . . . but you're not making this easy."

"Do you want me to leave? Take away the temptation?"

Maggie sat very still. The thought of his going struck her like a blow, making her slightly nauseous.

He misunderstood her silence, shoving away from the fence. "Damnit, is that what you really want?"

She opened her mouth to tell him maybe it would be best, knowing she needed to get away quick because she might throw up, but footsteps approached from behind them, cutting off her chance.

"Danny, Miz Dermott," Reggie Haskell said, tipping his hat in her direction. "If you're finished with this horse, I'd like to talk to you."

Danny gave her a hot glare and then relaxed his features, his easy grin sliding over his lips as he turned to Reggie. "I'm right behind you."

"See you at supper, boys," she bit out and quickly climbed off the fence. As she walked away, she had to concentrate to keep her strides even. Her knees felt weak. Her stomach roiled. How would she face him over the kitchen table later when the rest of the crew gathered in the kitchen for their meal?

She'd still worn the glow of their lovemaking in her cheeks at breakfast, but Danny had kept a nonstop conversation going among the hands, giving her privacy for her own thoughts as she'd bustled around the kitchen, serving up helpings of scrambled eggs and bacon, platters of fluffy biscuits and waffles.

Afterward he'd headed out with the men, giving her only a slow smile as he'd held the screen door open for a moment, and they'd share their only private glance.

She'd worn a smile long after she'd cleared away the dishes and begun preparations for bagged lunches the hands would take with them after they'd finished the morning chores.

He'd made it easy this morning, deflecting attention from her. Had he done it on purpose, or was he just acting on his own natural, *youthful* exuberance? That thought had chilled the lingering warmth his consideration had left.

Inside the house, she wandered back to the bedroom they'd shared. The scent of sex had dissipated from the air. But if she pulled back the covers and pressed her nose to the sheets, she knew she'd smell their blended aromas. She wanted to lift the covers and climb between them and drown in the memories.

A soft knock against the open door behind her made her jump.

Danny stood in the doorway, his intense gaze following hers to the bed. "The men are plannin' on goin' to town tonight. You don't have to worry about dinner."

Another reprieve. "Have fun," she said through stiff lips.

"Come with me."

She shook her head. Tears began to well in her eyes, and she turned away.

A soft curse behind her was all the warning she got before his hands clamped hard on her arms and he drew her around to face him.

His kiss wasn't the hard, angry taking she expected. She'd pushed him today. Rebuffed the attempt he'd made to reconnect with her. She expected some anger.

Instead he gently cupped the back of her head as his lips coaxed hers to let him inside.

Her hands crept slowly up his chest, fingers plucking at the thin cotton.

His tongue stroked over her mouth, prodding the seam of her lips until she opened for him.

Then it was too late to reconsider. Like the flick of a light switch, electricity arced instantly between them, and their bodies swayed together.

Maggie moaned into his mouth, slanting her head to deepen the kiss.

Danny's thigh slipped between hers. His hands clutched her bottom and brought her hard against the long, thick ridge riding under his zipper.

She broke the kiss just long enough to gasp, "The door."

Danny kicked back to shut it and then began to walk her toward the bed.

"We shouldn't," she whispered when they came up briefly for air.

"No one's around." Danny shoved her back and went to work on the buttons at the front of her blouse. "Reggie knows . . . gave me a stern talkin' to about bits and reins and not givin' a fine horse her head."

Maggie winced at that bit of news, but it didn't stop her from reaching for his shirt to pull the hem from his pants, working it up his chest until he had to stop what he was doing and strip it over his head.

Then he came at her again, yanking her shirt down her arms, opening her belt and pants with efficient flicks, and shoving her pants down to midthigh.

She wasn't as quick with his belt, because her fingers shook, so he pushed her hands away, grabbed her by the hips, and turned her, urging her to bend over the side of the bed.

With her jeans cinching her legs together, she wriggled, trying to reach behind her to push them off, but Danny stopped her by bracketing her thighs with his as he bent over her.

His cock nudged her folds, the hot, blunt tip of him poking, prodding until it found her opening.

When his hands came down on the mattress on either side of her, Maggie tensed, knowing this was going to come quick, fast . . . and, dear God, she hoped . . . *hard.*

Danny didn't disappoint, slamming straight between her folds, thrusting up her channel until his hard belly rested against her buttocks. He paused only a moment before pulling out and slamming forward again—so hard he jarred her whole body.

He did it again and again, slamming relentlessly against her, sharpening as his glides eased with the liquid her body released so that each thrust slapped loudly.

Maggie ignored the niggling worry that anyone outside her room, outside her house, would hear the noise they made: the unmistakable sound of flesh slapping flesh, growing moister, cruder, until the sounds themselves aroused.

"Maggie," Danny said, almost grunting, "am I getting it?"

He wasn't. Not that she didn't love what he did, but the curling tension inside her belly hadn't begun. "Doesn't matter," she muttered. "Don't stop."

Abruptly his cock pulled free.

She could have cried over the loss, but Danny didn't give her time to even moan. He flipped her over, tugged her pants and shoes off, and shoved her toward the center of the bed. Then he crawled up to join her, his jeans around his thighs, his slick cock reddened and engorged and looking so damn dangerous fresh arousal seeped from inside her.

He crawled between her legs, hooked his arms under her knees and pulled her ass off the bed.

Suspended on his arms, spread wide, with his cock sliding up and down her folds, she watched his jaw grind tight, his gaze hang on her sex, and Maggie had never felt sexier.

He drew his cock slowly down her slick folds and then pulled back his hips, pointed himself at her center, and began to circle as he entered her.

His slow screwing raked every inch of her channel. When he was all the way inside her, his gaze lifted, halting on her chest. "Open your bra," he said hoarsely.

"Can't, snap's behind me," she gasped.

"Then push it up. I wanna see you."

Her bra was an ugly, white appliance. Functional, sturdy. Necessary for someone of her proportions but embarrassingly unsexy. Still, pushing the wired cups over her breasts took some work and strained the portion of the breast she exposed.

Her nipples felt raw, but the cool air wafting over them soothed and excited.

His hot gaze excited her even more. "Touch yourself."

With his cock starting to stroke deep into her body again, her embarrassment eased. She wet her fingertips in her mouth and then brought them to her nipples and swirled them slowly over the tips.

A deep, growling groan rumbled from Danny's chest, and his arms tightened under her knees, jerking her closer. "You need friction, don't you, baby?" He pushed all the way inside and ground his groin against the top of her sex, scraping her clitoris. "You need it here?"

With her body beginning to melt and shiver, she nodded.

"Touch your clit," he whispered.

Her eyes widened, but she quickly slid one hand down her belly. Her arm pushed her breasts together, and Danny's breath hissed between his clenched teeth. His cock powered into her.

Her fingers slid through her creamy folds, seeking the tiny knot of nerves she'd learned a long time ago was the key to her pleasure. She toggled her middle finger over the rounded button and then swirled, toggled, and swirled, keeping her gaze locked on his face.

Release came quick and hard. Her back arched off the bed at the first faint ripple.

"That's it, baby," Danny said, excitement tightening his voice. He stroked harder, faster, and then, "*Jesus . . . fuck!*"

As her orgasm swept over in a hot, rolling wave, her legs straightened inside his arms, widening as she encouraged him to continue to thrust deep.

Danny fell forward still clutching her legs, pushing them upward, each thrust accompanied by a deep, masculine grunt, his face growing dark, strained, until, at last, his lips pulled away from his teeth and a long groan squeezed from his throat.

With cum shooting into her and Danny's strokes gradually easing, Maggie dragged deep breaths into her starved lungs and wrapped her arms around his shoulders, her urge to soothe and praise him so strong she had to clamp her lips shut.

Gazing at the ceiling, she realized she couldn't deny him. Couldn't turn her back to what was happening between them. For as long as he was here, she would welcome him—into her heart and into her body. She'd accept his loving as a gift. One she'd never expected, and would miss like an amputated limb when it was gone, but would treasure for as long as she lived.

Danny collapsed on top of her, still shuddering in the aftermath. "You'll come with me tonight," he said.

The lack of a rising inflection at the end of his statement made her smile. He lifted his head, eyes narrowed.

Maggie nodded slowly. "What should I wear?"

He'd asked her to wear a dress. She'd settled on a silky, floral number she'd never had the occasion to don. It swirled around her thighs and hips, didn't hug her soft middle, and still managed not to make her look terribly top-heavy.

Still, her breasts were where his gaze landed when she stepped off the porch.

"You look amazing," he said quietly. He held up the keys to his truck. "Would you mind driving?"

She lifted one brow. A man asking a woman to drive his big rig? Something was up. "Sure," she said easily, noting the little half smile that curved his lips.

Taking his keys, she climbed into the cab and strapped herself in and then waited while he did the same, cranking up the AC to cool the interior. "Rough day?" she asked innocently.

"I worked hard."

They shared a smile, and for once she didn't duck away as

heat filled her cheeks. "You know, we're going to get some strange looks."

He studied her for a moment. "Does it really bother you?" he asked quietly.

Maggie shrugged, edging away from the serious note. "I think I'm ready. It's just a date, right?"

His eyes narrowed. "Good." He lifted his chin toward the road. "Better get going. We're burnin' daylight."

Indeed, the sun balanced on the horizon like a big orange ball, painting the sky in thick strokes of mauve and purple. She pulled down the sun visor, turned the ignition, and pulled the truck onto the gravel road leading to the highway.

Once under way, she breathed deeply, doing her utmost to keep her eyes on the road.

He'd taken away her breath. Although he still wore cowboy Wranglers, his pale blue shirt with pearlized snap buttons lovingly hugged his wide chest and narrow waist. His dark hair was damp and starting to curl around his head. As tempting as those features were to savor, his eyes were what made her heart flutter. Deep, chocolate brown, they'd trailed her body as if she were a tasty snack.

From the corner of her eye, she watched Danny relax against the leather seat and turn slightly toward her. His hand settled on the seat close to her hip.

"Do you go to Honkytonk often?" she asked, trying to make conversation to infuse a casual mood and keep things light tonight. Yeah, she could do this. Go on a date with a younger man without looking like a complete fool—if she could just manage to keep him at arm's length.

"I like the place. Tara's good people."

"Tara Toomey? I've met her. I mean, I guess I've met everyone in town—it's not that big—but I don't know her well."

"You'll get the chance."

Suddenly his hand eased over her thigh, and her misgivings returned. "Um . . . Danny?"

"Does this distract you?"

"What do you think?"

He settled closer on the seat. "I think the road's straight . . . pretty empty. It's a fifteen-minute drive," his hand slipped between her legs, "and you smell good enough to eat."

The silky slide of his voice pricked her nipples into points. She licked her lips. "What do you have in mind?"

"Just keep your eyes on the road."

6

Danny knew he was being a devious bastard, but Maggie's refusal to commit to their relationship had forced his hand.

Knowing her stubborn little mind, she'd caved to his invitation while her mind had been muddled with passion, but she still held out hope she could control how deeply she slid toward surrender.

Perhaps she thought she could have her "little something" on the side, keeping secret just how close their relationship was.

However, he had other plans. Tonight there'd be no turning back, no denying she wasn't on the market for any other man to snap up.

In her pretty pink dress, she looked fresh and innocent, despite the maturity that softened her body. And she had no clue her soft brown eyes gave away her feelings every time her gaze landed on him. The woman was falling hard, and he'd make sure to give her another firm nudge toward the edge.

Even before they reached the saloon, he'd have her so turned inside-out she wouldn't be able to pretend their relationship was a casual thing. He'd keep her aroused, needy, responsive to every little touch of his hands and body. Anyone looking at them together would guess the truth. Then what could she say?

Already her breasts lifted against the silk. The thickness of her bra hid her dimpling nipples, but the rioting color adding blush to her cheeks and the skin above the rounded bodice of her dress told him what he would find if he slipped his hand inside.

Danny might be a few years shy of her ideal man, but he had a wealth of experience to share. Maggie would know soon enough she'd underestimated him.

His fingers glided in a lazy path up the inside her thigh. "What color panties are you wearing?"

A shocked laugh escaped her. "I beg your pardon?"

"Are they pink to match your dress?" he asked, remembering the pink pair she'd worn the first time he'd seen her naked.

"Guess you'll have to wait to find out," she said breathlessly.

"Don't know if I can do that, sweetheart. Wait, that is."

"But we're in the middle of the highway."

"The sun's going down. No one will see what we do if you pull the truck to the side of the road."

"I'm not having sex with you on a public road. Can't you wait? We just made—"

"You have a lot to learn about a young man's libido. And it's your own damn fault. One look at you in that pretty pink dress, and all I could think about were all the pretty pink things I want to kiss."

"Danny!"

His palm smoothed along her thigh, pulling up her skirt.

She closed her legs, trapping his hand. "Danny, I'm serious. Not here."

"Then pull up to that gate," he said, lifting his chin toward a small dirt road leading to a gate in the fence they passed.

"That's McKinnon's land."

"And he's probably sitting in his kitchen now eating his supper. Pull over." His hand slid higher between her tightly clasped thighs and cupped her sex.

She jerked the truck to the right, sliding in gravel as she came to halt at the gate.

Danny slipped out, opened it, and then waited while she sat in the cab. By the mutinous pout of her lips, he figured he had a fifty-fifty chance of walking home.

He held the gate and her stare, not breathing until she slowly pulled forward. He closed the gate behind them and climbed back into the cab. "Just behind those trees," he said, pointing toward three mesquites standing close together.

"Anyone looking will see the truck."

"They won't be looking. And we're cutting the lights."

"This is ridiculous!"

"We won't be long. Trust me?"

Maggie blew out an exasperated breath. "You've gotta be kidding. Every time you say that, you do something so wicked—"

"Aren't you dying to find out what I have in mind now?"

"I'm not getting naked with you here," she whispered furiously, bright color staining her cheeks.

"Won't have to," he drawled. "Just lift your skirt."

Her tongue slid out to wet her lips. "Are we going to do it right here? The steering wheel's in the way."

"How about we get out of the truck? We can stand on the side facing away from the road. No one will see a thing, even if they did happen to glance our way."

Maggie rolled her eyes. "I can't believe I'm letting you talk me into this."

"But you're going to do it, aren't you?"

She shot a glare his way and then opened her door and slid out, walking slowly around to join him as he jumped out eagerly.

When they faced each other, he lifted his hand and twirled his fingers, telling her silently to turn around.

With a heated huff, she faced the truck.

"You might want to hold on to something," he said silkily, stepping closer to slide his hands around her waist.

Although the sun had slipped below the horizon, the air was still hot. The light, floral scent she wore intensified in the heat, tickling his nose, inviting him to find every place she'd applied perfume to her skin.

He smoothed his hands around her belly and then glided them up to cup her breasts through her clothing. Right away, he knew he was going to change one little stipulation. He lifted her hair from the back of her neck and slowly pulled down her zipper.

"Thought you said I only had to lift my skirt."

"Can't help myself. I need to touch your breasts."

The dress opened, falling off her shoulders. He made quick work of the hooks at the back of her bra and slid the straps down her arms and then reached around to cup her large, firm breasts.

Her sigh was filled with blissful relief.

"You can't know how hard I get just thinking about touching you. You're so goddamn soft." He massaged her for a long time, waiting until her head fell back against his shoulder and her body leaned against him, pliant and relaxed.

Then he pulled up her skirt and reached underneath to snag the edge of her panties. He tugged them down, waiting as she stepped out of them, and then he tossed them through the window of the cab.

"Try not to wrinkle my dress," she whispered as he bunched it in his hands.

He snorted behind her but let down the fabric and rolled it carefully up. "That better?" he whispered.

Her nod was short, her body already tensing.

"Hold up your dress so my hands are free."

She did so, standing with her dress bunched around her waist, her chest bare, her bottom and sex exposed.

Danny smiled behind her. She was so eager, so curious, she didn't offer a single protest now. "Place one foot on the foot rail."

When she placed her sandal on the foot rail, he ran his hands down her outer thighs and then up again, smoothing around to come inside, stopping just below her pussy. "Open wider."

A soft, strained moan quivered from her lips, but she widened her stance, giving him access. His fingers traced her outer lips, feathering over her soft curls, and then tugged at the folds as he parted them. A moist sigh broke when he opened her damp, inner lips. He slid a finger inside her.

Her breaths deepened.

Looking over her shoulder, he could see her nipples beading, the areolae dimpling as he thrust his finger slowly in and out of her slick center.

"I can't believe you talked me into this."

"Funny how little you fussed about it."

"Guess I was curious."

"Hold on. Don't move."

Maggie held her skirts and her breath while Danny moved away. Suddenly he was crawling between her legs, coming up

144

under her, and sliding his back against the truck as he knelt between her legs.

His mouth was at just the right height. . . .

"Sweet Jesus. . . ." she breathed as his lips closed in, his tongue striking out to flutter against her clit.

Her fingers uncurled from around her skirt, and it drifted down to surround him. She braced one hand against the truck and lifted the other to her breast. She fondled herself as his mouth got down to the serious business of pleasuring her.

Danny had the knack, seemed to sense when she needed his fingers gliding deep and her clit stroked harder. Or maybe he simply listened as she begged.

"God, do that again. Deeper . . . oh!" Her knees wobbled, and she clutched the door handle to hold herself up as another sexy flicker of his tongue sent shivers through her thighs.

"Come for me," he rasped. "Don't hold back."

A short, painful laugh gusted from her. Hold back? Was he kidding?

His mouth drew on her clit, suckling hard, and Maggie jerked back her head, a moan ripping from her. A fluttering convulsion caressed the fingers sliding sinuously inside her.

As she came down from the precipice, Danny's hands caressed her bottom to soothe her, and Maggie wondered where the staid, rancher's wife was.

Unbelievably she stood in the middle of nowhere, her body mostly exposed to the warm air drifting over her heated skin, while a cowboy gave her oral sex.

A silly smile tilted her lips.

Danny drew away, crawled out from under her, and straightened. Then his calloused hands pulled the edges of her dress together and started tugging up the zipper.

"My bra," she said softly.

"Leave it off."

"I'll bounce."

"So long as you don't run from me, no one will notice."

"They'll see my nipples."

He snuggled close to her back, his arms enfolding her. "They'll be smashed against my chest while we dance, so they won't see a thing."

Maggie shook her head, sure he was going to drive her out of her mind. "Do you have an answer for everything?"

"Not to the most important question."

That stopped the retort she'd been ready to fling. She stepped off the foot rail and grimaced. "I'm wet."

He let her go, reached through the truck's window to swipe her undies from the seat, and held them out to her.

"I didn't bring a spare."

"I want you naked under that dress anyway."

She used the panties to clean up, shaking her head all the while. Life with Danny was sure full of surprises. Too bad it couldn't last.

Danny pulled into the parking lot in front of the bar in Honkytonk, cut the engine, and then cast Maggie a sideways glance.

The woman still fidgeted with the front of her dress, pulling at the fabric to try to loosen it around her breasts. When she saw him looking, she folded her arms over her chest.

"Are you gonna stay like that all evening?"

"I don't ever go without. I have reasons."

"I know. Two of them."

Her gaze narrowed on him, her lips pursed. "Why did I never notice this nasty side of you, Danny Tynan?"

"Never got me mad enough, I guess."

Her eyes rounded. "You're angry with me, but why?"

"Let's just go inside." When she started to let herself out of the truck, he drew in a deep breath. "Wait, let me get that for you."

"I can manage just fine on my own."

"Let me pretend I'm a gentleman."

"Fine." She pressed her lips together and waited while he got out and circled the vehicle.

When he opened the door, she turned sideways, holding her skirts firmly around her, and let him assist her from the truck.

"Still don't know why you could be mad," she grumbled. "I've let you do everything you wanted."

"Yes, you have," he said quietly.

She tugged at her bodice again.

"Stop that."

"But it's snug. It doesn't fit right without the bra."

"I like the way it looks. I can see your shape."

"Exactly!" She sighed and reached for the door handle. "Look, this isn't going to be any fun for you. Maybe I should take your truck home. You can catch a ride with one of the guys."

Danny pressed his mouth into a thin line and backed her up to the truck.

Her head tilted back as he crowded close, eyes glittering in the dark. Confusion creased the delicate skin between her brows.

He released a pent-up breath and pressed against her. "I'm sorry."

Her expression softened, unhappiness drawing down the corners of her lips. "What's wrong?"

"It's my problem. Not yours."

"Do I want to know what it is?"

One corner of his mouth quirked upward. "Definitely not. I'm feeling ornery."

Her head canted, and then her hand slipped between their

bodies, gliding up his thigh and cupping his erection. "Looks like a rather big problem," she said, a smile curving her lips. "Guess you'll have to walk close behind me."

"Very close."

"We don't have to stay long, do we?"

At the hopeful note in her voice, he wondered if she was eager to help him with his problem or just wanted an excuse to escape a public outing with him. "You still worried about what people will say?"

Maggie's lips twitched and then settled into a shy grin. "I'm thinking the ladies will be ready to scratch my eyes out."

He lifted one eyebrow. "The men are all gonna be sniffin' around your skirts."

Her finger traced the buttons down his shirt, stopping at his belt. Looking up from under the fringe of her thick lashes, she gave him a wink. "They'll be wondering what an old lady like me used for bait."

Dazed, Danny wondered when she'd gathered the reins. Somehow he was the one with the hard-on ready to eat bullets and follow her all night long like a lovesick puppy dog. He crooked his elbow and gritted his teeth. "Ready?"

She shook her head. "Not yet." Then she grabbed his shirt collar, stood on tiptoe, and kissed his mouth, putting the stamp on her ownership. "Let's get this over with," she said, staring unblinking into his eyes. "I'm already wishing we were heading back home."

Danny didn't think he'd ever really understand her. Hot and cold. Shy and then confident. He was beginning to think unraveling the mystery was a journey he never wanted to end.

Music blared through the old-fashioned double doors as they stepped onto the porch. Once inside, he scanned the crowd, found his quarry, and herded Maggie straight toward the bar.

Brandon Tynan glanced over his shoulder, and his mouth stretched into a wide smile. His gaze fell on Maggie and then snapped back.

Danny smiled and nodded. "Meet Maggie Dermott. Maggie, this is my brother, Brandon."

"Maggie, very nice to meet you," Brand said, holding out his hand.

When Maggie placed her hand inside Brand's, he kept it. "My brother giving you hell?"

Maggie laughed and gave Brand a pained look. "You know him better than me. What do you think?"

Brandon's smile widened. "I think you're doin' just fine." He let go of her hand and swung his arm around his brother's shoulder. "So, you gonna be my best man?"

Danny stood stock-still for a moment and then whooped, wrapping his arms around his brother to lift him off his feet. When he set him down, he lifted one eyebrow. "She ask you?"

Brand shook his head. "Can't say as I remember who did the askin'."

"Where's my new sister?"

"Gone to the ladies' room. She'll be right back."

Danny leaned over the bar. "Hey, Tara!" he shouted down the counter. "Did you hear?"

Tara Toomey turned from the customer she'd just smacked in the head and flashed a bright smile. "Did I hear? You think Lyssa could hold her pee for two seconds without tellin' me?"

She strode toward them, her gaze landing on Maggie. "Maggie Dermott, how the hell are ya?"

Maggie seemed surprised the woman knew her name. She gave Danny a quick, tight smile before answering. "I don't get away from the ranch much."

Danny watched the way Tara's glance went from Maggie to himself, saw the light dawning in her blue eyes. She blew a silent whistle. "Looks like we need drinks *all* the way around." Then she leaned across the bar toward Maggie and whispered loudly, "I'll need to see some ID."

Maggie pulled back, her eyebrows drawing together in confusion.

Tara shook her head. "Seeing as how I don't know you all that well, I have the right to ask."

"I promise I'm legal age to drink."

Tara lifted her chin and held out her hand.

Maggie's back stiffened, but she reached into the slim clutch she carried and took out her house keys with her license suspended from the chain in its leather and plastic carrier. She held it out to Tara, who pulled it toward her.

Maggie didn't let go, and Danny wondered if the two women were going to get into a tug-of-war over the license.

Brand shot him a glance, but Danny just shrugged, not knowing what Tara was up to.

Tara held the license at arm's length. "Well, well . . . that husband of yours was robbin' the cradle when he snatched you up."

"I beg your pardon?"

"I went to school with Douglas Dermott. And you look a whole lot younger than me. I was just curious," she said with a toothsome smile. "See you're dating someone at least within a decade of your own age now."

Maggie's swiftly indrawn breath had Danny reaching to snag her waist and pull her close before she turned to walk out the door.

Tara lifted her chin to Danny and then tossed him the license.

Maggie's hand shot up to grab it, but Danny's longer reach won out. He held it above her head while he turned it over to read.

When he glanced back at Maggie, he bit out, "Seven years?

That's all you're worried about? And here I thought you were a really well-preserved forty."

"Forty!"

"Well, thirty-five when the lights were low."

Her eyes narrowed, and she wriggled, trying to break his hold.

"You've had me jumping through hoops wonderin' how to get you past the embarrassment of being seen with me. Damnit, you're not even as old as my brother."

"Seven years is enough. Let me go."

"No way. Brand? Make sure our drinks don't walk off; me and the lady are gonna have a talk."

With his fingers biting into her waist, he forced her toward the dance floor where a three-man band played a slow ballad. He pulled Maggie around, clamped his arm around her back, and brought her up against his body—hard.

"So, Maggie-May, tell me what really bothers you about me."

7

Maggie tensed at the predatory glint in Danny's eyes as he drew her body flush with his. She would never call what they were doing "dancing." His body crowded closer than was decent in public, his thigh riding high between hers, his hands pressing on her ass to force her to ride it.

She struggled against him but gave up fighting when his expression turned downright mean. "I don't know what you're talking about," she said in a rush.

"Then think about it a minute. We've got all night." He pushed his thigh higher, pulling up her skirt. His hands forced her harder onto his thigh, and he began to shove her up and down.

The movements were shallow, not something anyone might notice unless they looked really close. The dance floor was dark enough she shouldn't have worried, but she didn't trust her own reactions not to give them away.

Friction burned hot between her legs, which added to the

sensitivity he'd left her with after their little tryst beside the road; Maggie feared she'd leave a wet spot on the front of her skirt.

"Don't do that," she whispered furiously.

"Do what? We're just dancing."

"You try to get off all the girls you dance with?"

"Miz Dermott, I can't believe that came out of your mouth."

The heated glare she aimed at him didn't make him flinch in the slightest. "All right," she said nastily. "You want to know what bothers me?"

Danny didn't answer, but he bent his head closer to hers.

Maggie quivered in his arms, telling herself it was anger but guessing she was only lying to herself. "You don't know me. I'm not this way—the way I am with you. When this thing burns out, what will I be left with? I'm not fool enough to think I'm some beauty who can hold tight to someone like you."

"You think I'm too pretty for you?"

"You're being silly now. You're not pretty. You're too manly, too virile. I'm just a chubby older woman. Nothing special. One day you'll wake up and look at me on your pillow and wonder what the heck you coulda been thinking."

Danny's nostrils flared, and he bent even closer. "If that isn't the most selfish thing I've ever heard," he said, his fingers biting into her flesh. "I guess you're right. I don't know you at all. I thought we were working on that. Getting to know each other, getting close. But you're so worried about your looks, all I can say is thank goodness you aren't a beauty or you'd be a total bitch, Maggie Dermott."

She jerked, and her body went rigid. Her breath gusted out in painful rush, leaving her shaking and slightly dizzy.

Danny's eyes widened, regret instantly softening his expression. "I didn't mean to say that," he whispered.

"I'm cutting in before you dig a deeper hole, little brother."

Maggie stood dazed as Brand waited beside his brother for him to release her and then gently took her hand and placed it on his shoulder.

Danny turned on his heels and walked away through the crowd, not looking back once.

"He cares about you, you know," Brand said softly.

Maggie dipped her head, blinking moisture from her eyes. "I know."

"He hasn't looked twice at any woman, long as I can remember. I was getting worried he wasn't all that interested until I saw the way he looked at you tonight."

"Don't tell me he hasn't been with other women. He knows too much for that to wash."

"Didn't say he didn't sleep with 'em. He's a man. He has needs. But he's never looked at a woman like she's precious."

Maggie closed her eyes and let Brand bring her closer to his chest. Her shoulders shook on a ragged indrawn breath. "He's special to me, too. I just think it's gone too fast. I want him to be sure."

"You may as well give up on him taking his time. He's determined to rush you right off your feet. Was it his idea or yours for you to lose your underwear?"

She stumbled over his foot and shot him a horrified glance. "You can tell?"

His gaze fell to her chest. "It's what I would have done."

"I'm gonna kill him." Heat flared in her cheeks.

A grin stretched his mouth. "I'm not sayin' you don't have to take it easy on him. Fact is, fightin's just an excuse to make up."

Maggie snorted, feeling better by the second. Danny had looked as stricken as she'd felt after he'd delivered his blistering set-down. She drew a deep breath and gave Brand a grateful smile. "Congratulations, by the way."

"Welcome to the family." He danced her toward the edge of the floor and then took her arm to guide her back to the bar where Danny stood beside Lyssa McDonough.

Both their heads were bent close.

"That can't be good," Brand muttered.

"Why's that?"

"The two of them, thick as thieves." He shot her a sideways glance. "They're plottin' something."

"Or comparing notes?"

"Maybe he's seekin' advice."

"About how to deal with me?"

"Then he's askin' the wrong woman," Brand said, his tone flat. "She's only good at gettin' into trouble."

"He doesn't need any help there."

They both broke into wide grins. "I think I like you, Maggie Dermott. You have a level head on your shoulders."

She bowed her head. "Thanks. I think."

"Let's go break this up."

As they approached, Lyssa and Danny were so engrossed they didn't notice, but Tara saw Brand and Maggie approaching and swatted Danny with a bar towel. Then she turned to give the two newcomers a broad smile. "All's fair."

Danny glanced up, his expression unreadable, but he pulled her under the crook of his arm. "I'm sorry about what I said," he whispered in her ear.

"Me, too." Then she pinched his waist hard and glared. "Your brother figured out I'm naked under this dress."

Danny chuckled, though tension still etched his face. "He's probably dying to know how you arrived in this state."

"Bet he's got a clue," she muttered and then fell silent, wondering if they'd done permanent damage to their budding relationship with the harsh words they'd exchanged. The thought frightened her more than she was willing to admit.

Maggie tilted her head. "Can we go home now?"

His gaze searched hers briefly. "Guess you're not having that much fun. Damn." Then he nodded. "Right," he said more loudly. "Early day tomorrow."

She couldn't stand the disappointment clouding his eyes, didn't like the way her own stomach roiled. She lifted her hand and placed her palm alongside Danny's cheek and then rose to press her lips to his.

"Right in front of God and everyone," he murmured when she drew away.

"Isn't this what you wanted?" she whispered. "For me to admit I want to be yours?"

His slow, sexy smile lifted the clouds surrounding her, and she grinned back.

"Leaving so soon?" Lyssa asked, her voice laced with sly humor. "You just got here."

"I think we're done here, don't you, Maggie?" Danny asked, his gaze never leaving hers.

Maggie's glance darted toward Brand and Lyssa, and heat crept into her cheeks at the fascinated stares she got from them.

"You'll have to come out to the ranch for dinner," Brand said. "Give us a chance to get to know you better."

"I'd like that," Maggie said, realizing it was true.

Danny tugged her hand—hard. "Let's go."

Maggie fluttered her fingers at the other couple and let Danny drag her through the crowd. She was going to have to talk to him about jerking her around; then again, he only got that abrupt when he was in a hurry to get her naked. She hoped like hell he'd let her wait until they were in the privacy of her bedroom.

Her bedroom. Not hers and Doug's. The first time she'd thought of it that way.

Well, hell. Maybe she really was ready to let go at last. Explore this new relationship with this inappropriate man.

"You've got it all wrong, you know," Danny said quietly on the ride home.

"What are you talking about?"

"Me and you. This doesn't have anything to do with who's got years on the other person. You think you owe Douglas to be miserable."

She sucked in a harsh breath. "That was a little brutal."

"I don't know any other way to say it. Things didn't go well for the two of you. Maybe you even thought you needed to get out of the marriage, but you never got the chance for a clean break, did you?"

Maggie stared out the window. That wasn't a place she liked to go in her mind—too much guilt and sorrow dwelt there. "I never thought about divorce, but I wasn't happy. Maybe there just wasn't time to figure out that's what I wanted. I'd just faced the fact I wasn't happy, and then he got sick."

"What was wrong with him?"

"Prostate cancer."

"That's why you didn't have kids?"

"He was already sterile by the time they found it."

"You couldn't leave him then."

"Wouldn't even have considered it. As horrible as it was for him, I felt like God was punishing me, too."

"Maggie . . ."

"It's all right. It's just survivor's guilt. But for the longest time, I didn't think I deserved to be happy."

"Come over here. You're too far away."

Maggie unbuckled her belt and slid along the seat, feeling under her hip, and his, for the center seat belt and then fastening it around her waist before she settled beside him with her head on his shoulder.

157

"I'm truly sorry, Maggie. As soon as the words were out of my mouth, I wanted to kick my own ass."

She reached up and pressed a finger against his lips. "It's done. We both feel like jerks." She snuggled deeper against him and sighed. "This is nice."

"Don't get too comfortable."

The sexy slide of his voice made her smile. "Don't want me falling asleep on you?"

"Think it's even possible?"

"Maybe I'll wear you out this time."

"I'd sure like watchin' you try."

Their lovemaking was different this time.

They started slowly, undressing without the usual rush, pressing intimate kisses as they bared their skin and hearts. When Danny finally rose on his arms above her and thrust inside her body, Maggie knew she'd never felt this full, this complete. He'd chased all the shadows from her soul, replacing them with hope for a future filled with all the things she'd ever yearned for—home, family, a man who would love her through all the trials they'd face.

How had it happened so quickly? She didn't realize she'd said it out loud until Danny growled above her.

"You think this was quick? I've been waitin' seven years for the time to be right."

"You loved me even then?"

"I was crushin' hard. Too young to know better."

"It's just as well. The circumstances needed to be right, or we would never have felt good about it."

His mouth swooped down for a deep, wet kiss that left her toes curling in the air.

"Will I scare you if I tell you I'm halfway to being in love with you already?"

"Your love won't ever scare me, Maggie."

She tightened her arms and legs around him, undulating her hips to encourage him to move faster.

"I won't ever get tired of this," he growled. "Bein' inside you. Your soft body under me."

"Funny, it's all your hard places that make me weak."

A wry, pained smile curved his lips. "You know it's not natural for a man to talk this much when he's fuckin'."

"I so love it when you talk dirty."

"That why you're blushing?"

"No, I'm thinking about what I'd like you to do to me."

"Now? More than this?"

"Uh-huh." She drove her hips upward, swallowing his cock with a sexy glide. "I've been wondering what the view's like from on top."

"You want to try it? Even when things start to jiggle that embarrass you?"

She didn't get a chance to do more than nod before he rolled them both. When she caught her breath, she was straddling his body, his cock still locked inside her.

Pushing against his chest, she straightened, enjoying the way the action drove his hardness deeper inside her body. "This all right for you?" she asked, giving an experimental little stroke. "I know how you like to be in charge."

"I'm lovin' the view. Keeps my hands free, too," he said, reaching up to cup her breasts.

"I should have known that's what you'd go for."

"Don't want you hurting anything when you start to bounce."

"I'm not going to bounce," she teased. "I'm more graceful than that."

"Baby, I can promise you won't be able to resist." His hands slid around to grasp her buttocks, and he silently encouraged her to rise on her knees and then come down again.

Maggie shuddered, discovering very quickly just the right angle and speed to build the friction between her inner walls and his thick shaft. Soon she was laboring above him, her breaths getting short and ragged, her fingers digging into his chest as she shoved up and down.

She couldn't move fast enough, couldn't draw in deep enough breaths to maintain the fiercely rocking motions that sped her toward her orgasm. "Danny . . ." she groaned. "Please."

"It's okay. Lift up a bit." His head dug into the mattress, and he bent his knees and pumped his hips upward, spearing into her, his hands bracketing her hips to keep her poised above him.

Maggie, still braced against his chest, leaned over him, adjusting to take his upward thrusts, gritting her teeth as his groin hit her clit.

Sweat beaded on her forehead and upper lip, trickled between her breasts, and still she held on, silently giving thanks for his stamina as tension wound itself around her womb, tightening her thighs and belly until her body arched and her orgasm swept through her.

Danny continued to pump despite the burning in his thighs and buttocks. As Maggie let go, her mouth slackening around an anguished moan, her eyes squeezing tight, he was free to fill his mind with the sight of her. He'd never tell her, but her sweet, pillowy breasts *jiggled* with every hard thrust he delivered.

At last, she wilted, falling toward his chest, and he relaxed beneath her, resigned that his own release would be a while in coming.

Her cheek rubbed his shoulder like a kitten.

Danny sank his hand into her hair and held her close, loving the gentle ripples that squeezed his cock as her orgasm slowly faded.

"I love this part," she murmured.

"So do I."

"Sorry," she moaned. "I fell down on the job."

He smiled against her hair, even while fighting the urgent, painful fullness that made him want to flip her onto her back to find his own release. "I don't mind," he said truthfully. "It's not terminal."

"Would you like me to help?"

"You've already helped quite a lot," he said, pretending not to understand.

"I mean. I could go down on you," she whispered.

"Well, I guess. If you don't mind. But I have to warn you, I probably won't last two seconds I'm so hard."

As she slowly slid down his body, he reached down and wrapped his fingers around the base of his cock, determined to wring as much pleasure from the experience as he could manage before he lost his mind.

The phone rang in the early morning hours. Maggie reached sleepily over Danny's body and brought the phone to her ear. "Hello?"

"Maggie. I need to talk to Danny."

Recognizing Brandon Tynan's deep timbre immediately, she became instantly alert. The tightness of his voice told her there was trouble.

"Danny," she whispered, shaking his shoulder. "Brand's on the phone."

"Wha—" He grabbed the phone from her, scraped his hand over his face, and sat up. "Brand? What's happened?"

Maggie watched as his eyes widened and he sucked in a

deep, charged breath. "Soon as I pack, I'll be on my way." He handed the phone to Maggie, scooted off the bed, and headed straight for the door.

She hung up the phone and trailed behind him, watching silently as he emptied the drawers of his dresser and tossed clothes at the bed. "What's the matter? What's happened?"

His jaw tightened, and he flashed her a glance filled with anguish. "Mac McDonough's unit got hit yesterday by an IED. The army's already medevaced him to Germany. He'll be in Walter Reed tomorrow. I have to go home."

Maggie nodded and headed to his closet, dragging out his black duffel. "Go shower. I'll finish packing for you," she said, not looking up.

When he headed to the bathroom, she efficiently folded away his clothing, trying not to think beyond the task at hand, trying not worry about herself and where this left their relationship.

She shut out the thought that he hadn't even considered what his leaving would mean to her—that he planned to get into his truck and drive away without giving her a hint where their relationship was headed.

And she wouldn't ask, because she'd add another burden.

Instead she slipped on her robe, headed to the kitchen, started coffee brewing, and cut thick slices of homemade bread, which she toasted and buttered.

When he strode through the kitchen, she had everything bagged, ready for him to take with him on his journey back to his old life. "Why aren't you dressed?" he asked hoarsely.

Her heart leaped inside her chest. "I thought . . ." She didn't know really know what she thought, so she let her voice trail away.

"I need you with me, Maggie. Were you really gonna let me walk out of here by myself?"

"I didn't want to intrude."

"Damnit, I don't want you polite. I want you packed."

"I'll go get ready," she said, not minding his anger in the least.

She ran down the hallway, grabbed a suitcase from her closet, and opened drawers to dump her clothes into the bag, not caring whether she had anything packed that made sense for her destination.

"You goin' in your nightgown?"

She glanced up to the doorway, saw him standing with his hands braced on either side, and then followed his glare to her own body. "I'll shower when I get there," she whispered.

"I'll get this to the car and let Reggie know we're out of here."

Five minutes later they were pulling away from her home, heading to the McDonough's ranch.

"Are you sure they won't mind my coming? They don't really know me."

"You're with me. That's all they need to know." He reached for her hand. "I thought we had time for this. To get you used to the idea of being with me. Now everything's comin' fast. You okay with that?"

"Danny . . ." She laid her head on his shoulder. "I guess if I had more time, I just might come up with more excuses why we shouldn't. Maybe this is the way it's supposed to happen."

"Why don't you take a nap. We'll be there in about forty minutes? I'll wake you when we get there."

"Did they say whether Mac would be okay?"

"They don't know much right now, just that he's doing well enough to be moved back to the States. That has to be good, right?"

She didn't reply—just snuggled closer to his shoulder. "We'll just have to wait and see."

After several quiet minutes, Danny cleared his throat. "I'm glad you're with me. I really thought you'd make some excuse to stay behind."

"And there I was feeling down because you didn't ask me to come."

Danny snorted. "What's the lesson here?"

"That we should talk about what we're thinking because we probably won't ever get it right?"

"I don't think that's it," he said drily. "You stick close to me, and we'll be just fine."

"I think that's something I don't have to give much thought to." She yawned and let her eyes slide closed.

Danny glanced down at Maggie's head as she nodded off to sleep, a mixture of emotions roiling inside him: Gratitude for finally hooking up with the one woman who made his heart smile. Fear for what was coming for his friends and family.

He had to have faith that somehow everything would work out just as it was supposed to. He had proof lying against him that love always found a way.

Straight Up Soldier

1

Mac McDonough's body ached with the need to sink into soft, wet *woman*.

An escape, no matter how brief, from the constant throbbing in his shattered leg.

Like an answer to his prayer, a familiar SUV crawled up the rough gravel road. His body tightened. Tara Toomey had offered the last time she paid him a visit, for old time's sake, but he'd turned her down because he'd still had just enough pride and just enough affection for his old friend not to want to use her like that.

Today she wouldn't make it past the door. The thought of her blond flyaway curls wrapped around his dick made him throb with anticipation.

As she slowly made her way up the winding, rutted road, Mac McDonough closed his eyes and turned his face into the gusting, humid air and inhaled the fresh scent of the coming rain—a fierce reminder of just how far he'd come.

Over seven thousand miles and another lifetime.

The cabin, nestled high on a ridge overlooking hills covered with live oak and cedar, seemed as far removed from his version of reality as the face of Mars.

Sure, the ground was a bed of sand and rock, but the sand was grittier, the grains larger than the wheat flour a Hummer could kick up into the air, leaving a trail that could be tracked for miles across the desert floor.

The air was almost as hot but filled with so much moisture it felt thick as he dragged it deep into his lungs.

Mac curled his fingers around the porch rail and leaned into it, savoring the solitude he'd needed to heal his soul—a solitude with which no amount of therapy or medicine could compare.

The only thing missing from the picture was another case of whiskey to help him sink into a stupor, easing the pain-filled tension in his body and shutting out the memories that haunted his dreams.

And a woman. Not that he was willing to leave the cabin to go on the prowl for one, but the longer he remained in his self-imposed isolation, the more urgent became the need. Any woman would do—so long as she didn't want to talk, didn't want to be wooed. He hadn't the time or the heart left for either.

However, if all Tara offered him this go-round was whiskey, he might make it through another week before he lost his mind.

The silver SUV ground to a halt. Tara slammed open her door and jumped down from the cab, her arms already opening wide as she approached.

He stiffened automatically as her embrace surrounded him, and then he forced himself to relax. "Tara, let's get it on," he growled.

Tara flung back her head and laughed. "Soldier boy, that's the least appealing proposition I've gotten today."

His arms clamped hard around her lean body. "I'm not kidding. Right here, right now. Let's do it."

Her blue eyes clung to his face, and her smile dimmed for just a moment before stretching wide again. "You're in a bad way, aren't you?"

"You gotta ask?" he said, rutting his groin crudely against her soft belly.

Air whistled through her pursed lips. "Now, there's something I don't feel every day. Almost forgot you come packin' some *serious* hardware."

"Is that a yes?" he bit out irritably.

Tara gave him another hug and then eased out of his arms. "As tempting as your offer is, I'm gonna have to say no. I'm saving myself these days."

He lifted an eyebrow, not missing the slight blush that painted her cheeks a pretty rose. "Well, fuck."

She laughed again and whirled, heading back to her vehicle. "Go get off that leg. I brought gifts. We'll talk."

Mac cussed again. The last thing he wanted to do was talk. About anything. Especially about anything to do with his returning home. He wasn't ready.

Fact was, he didn't know if he ever would be.

He gathered the cane he'd left leaning against the rail and limped into the cabin, heading for the lounge chair and the overstuffed ottoman that had served as his bed more times than the mattress in the cozy room at the back of the one-bedroom cabin Tara had lent him.

Tara returned with two grocery bags and set them on the kitchen table. She hummed as she put away her purchases in the cupboard, and Mac closed his eyes, pretending to nap.

When something cold touched his fingers, he peeked from beneath his eyelids and gratefully accepted the tumbler with a double shot of whiskey on ice.

He raised his glass and gave her a glare that had her chuckling as she took a seat on the small sofa opposite him.

"A toast," she said, raising her own glass.

"What are we celebrating?" he said, determined to make the effort to be polite, even though his "condition" still screamed for attention.

"To friends," she replied, her gaze sliding away.

Suspicion raised hackles on the back of his neck, but he remained silent, watching Tara fidget on the sofa as she sought the right words to start the conversation.

He sighed, knowing he had to show polite interest. "Lyssa and Brand set a date?"

"They're waiting for you."

Mac's lips twisted. "Tell her to plan it. I'll walk her down the damn aisle."

"They want you home first. To stay."

"Thought Brand had everything under control. They have any more problems with smugglers?"

"No signs lately. DEA and the rangers scoured the place and set up patrols up and down this side of the river. They think the bastards moved their route."

Mac eased back in his chair. "Then he's got it covered."

"They're both run pretty ragged. Brand's got his own spread to manage; Lyssa's working yours. Of course, they're not getting much sleep."

Mac grimaced, knowing exactly why his baby sister wasn't getting any rest. "Danny still back at Wasp Creek with his woman?"

Tara nodded; a smile stretched her mouth. "He's got his

hands full. Maggie's pregnant, and he's decided to pitch in to run her place."

"Pregnant? Is he marrying her?"

"They did it last weekend at the saloon."

A pang of regret tightened his chest. In that other lifetime, he would have been there. "Good for him."

"Mac . . ."

He tensed, knowing she was finally getting to the point of the visit and girding himself to refuse. Saying no to family or Tara tore him up, but he just wasn't ready to reenter that world again.

Too many shadows hovered around him. He felt too tense, too rangy. His mood swings still verged on dangerous. Habits he'd picked up in the desert—instincts he couldn't turn off— left him feeling out of control of his reactions and emotions.

Maybe if he could get a good night's sleep, just once, without the aid of alcohol . . .

Just one night. . . .

"Go ahead and spit it out," Mac ground out. "I'll tell you no. You can nag me to death until you go. Then you can tell the folks at home you tried. But, Tara, I'm not going back. Not yet."

"This is something else. . . ." The quiet tension in her voice caught his attention "And I don't know who else to ask."

He stared into the glass, not willing to see the plea in her blue eyes. "What is it?"

"I have this friend who's in trouble. Her ex-boyfriend's gonna kill her."

Heavy, dark clouds cloaked the late afternoon sun. Wind whipped the lake's surface into white, foamy peaks that lapped rhythmically against the long pier.

Mac skirted the boat dock, sparing only a glance at the ducks, wings tucked close their bodies, bobbing on choppy waves. He'd parked along a dirt trail and hiked in, wanting to get the lay of the land and see just how prepared for danger the woman was.

If he didn't get his ass peppered with bird shot, he planned to give the stubborn fool the fright of her life and send her packing somewhere safe, somewhere law enforcement could do its job.

He'd have things wrapped up here in just a few minutes and head back to the cabin to ice his aching leg, content that he'd taken care of Tara's friend. Then maybe she'd leave him the hell alone.

With an eye toward natural concealment, Mac scanned the trail leading up to the woman's small vacation home. Trees hid the view of the dock. Anyone in a boat could tie off and make it all the way to the small clearing surrounding the cabin before he'd be seen.

He pushed aside a branch and peered into the clearing. The small stone and wood cabin sat nestled at the center. Surrounding the weathered structure was grass gone to seed. Overgrown rosebushes sprawled against the porch, heavy red blossoms weighing down the leggy stems so the petals fell like droplets of blood across the front steps.

The front door stood wide open.

An overturned bucket lay in front of the door, and water dripped down the porch steps.

His heart thudded in his chest, and he reached behind him for the Glock he'd tucked into his pants.

Maybe he was already too late. Just like Baghdad.

He'd told Tara he was the wrong man for the job. Hell, these days he didn't feel like much of a man at all.

Gritting his teeth against the pain, he crouched low, praying his knee wouldn't collapse and pitch him into a sprawl on his face. He then made his way as quickly as he could to the side of the cabin.

Except for the sifting wind and the endlessly lapping waves, silence fell around him. His heartbeats slowed, his breaths evened out, and, once again, he was outside the Green Zone, stalking unknown horrors through dusty, littered streets.

Mac shook his head to clear his thoughts, focusing on now, on the woman Tara had described as a "babe in the woods"—so unprepared for what was happening she'd fled a safe house for the relative openness of her vacation refuge.

One her stalker knew all too well.

Mac climbed the porch at the side of the house, dragging his healing leg up each step. Then he pressed his back against the pale yellow siding and made his way carefully toward the front door, peering around window casings into the shadowed interior for signs of an intruder.

At the doorway, he raised his weapon chest high, sighting down the barrel as he quickly turned the corner and entered the house.

A crash toward the back had him hurrying as best he could, stopping at each doorway to make sure each room was clear before he arrived at a brightly lit kitchen.

Pausing just outside, he sucked in a deep breath and then rounded the corner, his weapon pointing straight ahead.

He drew down on a woman whose wide, frightened eyes stared at him over the barrel of a shotgun.

Shit! Mac turned his weapon toward the ceiling and raised his left hand. "I'm not going to hurt you."

Suki Reese's tongue swept out to wet her lips. Her stare never wavered. "Put the gun on the floor in front of you, or I promise you'll have a hole where your heart beats now."

For some inexplicable reason, that line amused him, tugging

at the corners of his lips. "Bending that far might be a problem."

A frown formed a crease between her brows. "Why's that?"

"My leg's got pins holding the bones together. I don't bend."

Her gaze glanced quickly down his body. "You made it fine this far."

Mac gave a slight shake of his head. "Pure adrenaline got me here. Saw the bucket overturned on the porch. Thought I might be too late."

"I dropped it when I heard you coming."

He snorted. "Did I make that much noise? Must be losing it."

"I'm a little jumpy. Any sound at all . . ."

Something Mac could definitely relate to.

Her eyes narrowed further, and her fingers tightened around her gun. "*Who are you?*"

He eyed her rigid tension, hoping she really did know her way around a gun. "Mac McDonough. Tara Toomey sent me to fetch you."

Her brows shot high. "*Fetch* me?"

He nodded slowly.

"I'm doing just fine on my own. So you can head out the way you came."

"How about we talk?" Mac couldn't believe he'd just said that. To a woman drawing down on him. "Do you even know how to use that peashooter?"

"I chambered two shells while you shuffled down my hallway. And you're so close it won't matter if I don't hit exactly where I aim."

Mac nodded. "Guess you do know how." Keeping his expression as unthreatening as he could, given the scar streaking down one cheek, he said, "Look, my leg feels like it's on fire. Can I take a seat?"

Her expression underwent a subtle shift. Worry drew her brows together while her eyes narrowed further. She took two cautious steps toward him. "Hold the stock by your thumb and forefinger and hand the gun to me."

Despite the ache in his leg, Mac was starting to enjoy the situation, even saw the humor in the fact a woman had gotten the drop on a soldier who'd survived months living by his wits in a war zone.

It also didn't hurt that she was easy on the eyes.

Of mixed Anglo-Asian descent, her glossy black hair fell to just below her chin. Large, almond-shaped eyes glittered with deadly intent. Her lips pressed together but still managed to pout; her upper lip was full and bowed. Her skin seemed unnaturally white—as though the blood had drained from her face from fright.

Damn Tara anyway. She'd known exactly what she was doing when she'd turned him down. The ache in his leg paled now in comparison to the uncomfortable fullness in his groin.

Mac shrugged, turned his weapon slowly, and held it out for her to snatch away. Unarmed, he turned his back on her, trusting she wouldn't change her mind and put a "hole where his heart beat" while he walked unsteadily to a kitchen chair.

He'd left his cane in his rented car. Thought he'd be back in minutes and could gut out the discomfort. Looked like he was here for at least as long as it took to talk some sense into the stubborn woman.

Lowering himself slowly, he waited while she edged toward the phone on the counter, hit the speaker button, and then another speed-dial number.

Tara's cheerful voice answered moments later, music playing in the background. "Honkytonk Bar, how can I help you?"

"Tara?" Suki began, an irritated edge in her tone.

"Suki! Did Mac make it over there before dark?"

Suki's frown deepened into a dark scowl. "You knew he was coming?"

"Describe him, just to be safe."

Suki rolled her eyes and then swept Mac slowly with her pointed gaze. "Over six feet tall—"

"Six-three," he said silkily, warming to the exchange.

"Dark brown hair with glints of red, cut short like a marine."

"I'm not a damn jarhead," he growled.

"Sour disposition. Bossy as hell. Needs to shave. Oh, and walks with a limp."

"That's him, all right. Didn't I call to tell you he was on his way?"

"No."

Tara's snort was pure theater. "I thought I had. Must have gotten busy. You didn't shoot him or anything, did you?"

Suki hit the OFF button and at last lowered her gun. "Guess you're who you say you are," she muttered. "Now get the hell out of here."

Mac stared steadily at the woman who seemed just as determined as he was, or had been, to go it alone. Taking a closer look, he noted the deep shadows under her eyes and the slight tremor of her hand as she set the weapon on the counter and flipped on the safety.

She was too thin, her movements just a little jerky. She was at the end of her strength and badly in need of rest and relief from constant fear.

Again, something he understood only too well. But he sat square in the middle of Texas, not Tikrit or Baghdad. It was a goddamn crime a woman should be scared out of her mind by some asshole who didn't have the *cojones* to face her in the open or the right mind to just let her go.

Mac drew a deep breath, arguing good and loud with himself about the merits of getting involved with someone else's little war when he hadn't managed to throw off the shadows that haunted him from the war he'd been ripped from three months earlier.

"Suki, have a seat. I'm not going anywhere. We need to talk."

2

The last thing Suki Reese needed was another man telling her how it was going to be. Her head pounded like thunder, she hadn't been able to get a decent night's sleep in days, and her stomach was so tense she thought she might throw up on Mac McDonough's pointy leather boots. She'd lived on nerves and caffeine for the past week and felt ready to pass out.

This had been her reality since she'd found the note pinned to her hotel-room door. No matter how hard the officers assigned to watch her argued, she'd quietly packed her bags and fled San Antonio for the comfort of her little cabin in the woods.

She'd made only two phone calls since then: one to the officer in charge of the investigation into her boyfriend's Mexican mafia connections, and one to Tara Toomey. She hadn't known who else to call, who else might know someone who could get her out of this mess—or at least give her peace of mind so she could rest and plan her next steps.

The man sitting in front of her, massaging his leg, didn't look like the answer to her prayers.

For one thing, he was too menacing—another hulking man who dwarfed her petite form. Admittedly, he was her preferred "type," until she'd gotten involved with Manny Menchaca. The long, jagged scar on Mac's cheek, the scruffy beard, and his dark, brooding expression made her quiver.

Not that he wasn't handsome underneath the macho crap. Broad shoulders and bulging biceps stretched his brown tee. Faded, fraying jeans hugged hips and thighs that would have made her sigh a few months ago. Add that to his piercing green eyes and rugged, sharp-edged features, and she ought to be drooling. Instead she noted the haggard lines pinching the sides of his lips and the pain that deepened the crease between his frowning eyes, and an unexpected surge of empathy flooded her.

"You okay?" she asked quietly as she leaned against the counter behind her.

"Sit," he bit out. "Let's talk."

Not ready to get too close, she hedged. "Want coffee?"

"Got anything stronger?" She shook her head. "Shit. Coffee will have to do."

She busied herself drawing water from the faucet and setting the pot to brew before she faced him again.

"Why this place?" he asked in his clipped fashion.

"Why not? Wasn't like the safe house the cops provided worked out." She shrugged. "I like it here. I know it. I thought I might be able to relax a bit."

"You don't think he'll follow you here?"

She shrugged. "I know he will. Once he figures it out."

"Tell me, are the police interested only because he's stalking you?"

"They're interested because he's connected to drug runners.

DEA was ready to pull him in, but he escaped across the border."

"If he knows they're after him, why would he bother coming back?"

A bitter smile curved the corners of her lips. "He doesn't take rejection well." Her gaze fell to his leg. "What's wrong with you anyway?"

"My leg was blown to hell a few months back. I'm still recovering."

Curiosity burned inside her, but she really didn't want to get too friendly and share too many secrets with the man. Not when she just wanted him to leave. "I know Tara's trying to help, but don't you think you should be somewhere taking it easy?"

Mac's smile wasn't amused. "It's true, I didn't want to come. Tara asked me as a favor. If I had my choice, I'd be sitting back at my place with Jim Beam right now."

"I don't know what she was thinking. . . ."

"Didn't you ask her for help?"

"Yes," she said slowly, "but you're not what I had in mind."

His green gaze sharpened. "Because of my leg?"

"No, because you're too . . ." Heat crept across her cheeks. "You're too big."

His expression remained unchanged—stayed watchful, slightly amused. "Do I frighten you?"

She swallowed and then nodded. Better not let on about the other feeling.

"Did this Manny hurt you?"

The little strength holding her straight ebbed away, and she clutched the counter.

"Goddamn," he said softly and then pushed up from his seat and walked toward her.

Suki's eyes widened, and she shrank back.

However, he simply held out his hand to cup her elbow and pulled her toward the table, waiting as she sat in the seat he'd vacated. "You look ready to pass out. I'll get the coffee."

Tears filled her eyes, and she blinked rapidly.

Mac limped around the kitchen while searching cupboards for cups. Then he poured coffee and returned, one cup at a time in his hand. The set of his jaw told her he had to concentrate, and she wondered how difficult it was to balance a cup of coffee, given his injury.

Another twinge of sympathy tickled inside her. He'd said his leg was "blown to hell." The wording of that statement and the camo-brown tee made her wonder if he was in the military.

Certainly looked the type. Made sense Tara would send someone like him to watch over her. Still, Suki wished he wasn't so intimidating.

He brought over the second cup, hooked his hand around a chair back, and turned it to settle onto it backward, his legs spread wide around the sides. "What are your plans?"

"Besides not getting killed?"

He took a sip and narrowed his gaze. "Were you planning on staying here until he finds you?"

She shrugged. "The law-enforcement guys know where I am. They want him pretty bad, so I imagine they're scrambling to see who keeps watch. Hopefully they'll grab him before he gets to me."

"No one stopped me coming in. Must still be drawing straws. Are they using you as bait?"

"Looks like it." She wrapped her fingers around the steaming cup to stem the telltale tremors and forced her voice to remain even. "They didn't seem surprised when he tacked a love letter to the door of my last hiding place."

Mac's lips thinned, and his dark brows lowered. "I'm staying, but I didn't come prepared for a siege. I'll have to send for some things. Clothes, and you won't have enough food stocked for both of us."

Suki shook her head, alarm making her heart thud dully in her chest. "I don't want you here. I'll manage on my own. The cops will be all over this place soon."

Mac took another slow sip and then set his cup on the table. "Do you have more than one bedroom in this place, or do I get the couch?"

Suki stared. "Didn't you hear what I said?"

"I heard you, all right. I just choose not to respond."

Though his tone was nonchalant, she heard the underlying steel. Mac wasn't going to budge, and the thought made her tremble.

"Put your head down."

"What?"

"Put your head between your knees. You look ready to slide onto the floor."

"I'm not going to faint," she muttered.

"Look, I'm not going to hurt you."

"I don't want you here."

"I heard you the first time."

"Why are you doing this?" she whispered.

Mac's lips pressed together, and his piercing eyes grew haunted. "Because I know what it's like to be scared. You look like you haven't really slept in days. Let me give you that— peace of mind—so you can rest."

"You think I can sleep with you under my roof?"

"Sleep hugging that shotgun if you like, but I'll be outside your door. No one's getting past me."

Hope flared in her chest, and tears slid down her cheeks. Sleep. God, could she? "Just tonight then?"

He paused; a muscle alongside his jaws flexed as he ground them together. "Tonight you're getting some rest."

She blinked dully and then rose from her seat, not bothering to look back to see what he did. Tara wouldn't send someone who would hurt her. Snatching the shotgun from the counter, she headed out of the room and down the corridor to her bedroom. Once inside the door, she locked it.

She crawled onto the mattress, rested the shotgun on the bed beside her like a lover, and closed her eyes. No way could she rest with Mac roaming through her house, but she didn't have the strength left to spar with him.

For now, just lying still in the quiet room was enough. She ought to be grateful to him. He'd given her something else to obsess over.

A tall, hard body. Brooding, implacable expression. She almost felt sorry for Manny.

Mac stepped onto the porch, and pain sliced through his leg, hot and fierce. He sucked air between his clenched teeth in a furious hiss.

He'd walked farther than he had the last time he'd used the treadmill at the VA hospital, and over uneven ground. The dull ache he'd complained to Suki about was a pulsing agony now.

But he had his duffel and his cane. As he'd walked back to the cabin, leaning on it, he'd thought that maybe seeing the cane would help Suki accept that while he was "too big," he wasn't invulnerable.

The look that had shattered her expression when he'd asked whether her asshole ex-boyfriend had hurt her still cut him to the bone.

Entering her home, he tugged the door closed against the gusting wind and flipped on the outside light switch, deciding that the porch light streaming through the window would provide enough illumination for him to make his way through the house. Better to be safe and keep the interior in darkness in case prying eyes peered inside.

He settled onto the sofa, slid sideways, and used both hands to lift his leg onto the cushion. Then he bent to rifle through his duffel for his cell phone.

He found it, flipped it open, and hit REDIAL. As soon as music blared, he said in a loud whisper, "Tara!"

"That you, Mac?" she shouted.

"Get somewhere you don't have to shout to be heard."

Several moments later, Tara was back. "How is she?"

"Safe. Sleeping, I hope. She's a wreck."

"Poor thing," she replied softly. "She's really been through it."

Mac rubbed the bridge of his nose. "Tell me about her."

"Thought you were just going to do a drive-by, make sure she was safe, and then head on your merry way."

He didn't miss the amusement lacing her sultry voice. "You set me up."

"Sure did. Feel sucker punched?"

"Something like that."

"She's a sweet girl."

Sweet? He hadn't seen that side yet. Just the sexy, wounded woman who tore at his sense of honor. "How do you know her?"

"She worked for one of my distributors. A sales rep. Has been servicing the account for years."

"Why's she special to you?"

"You've met her. She's lovely, smart."

"And?"

"We've been to a couple of conventions together, shared a room once. Doesn't snore."

He shook his head. Tara picked up strays like old ladies picked up kittens. "What do you know about the bastard stalking her?"

"Nasty character. Smooth-talkin' Romeo. Seduced her right off her feet, but when he started showing his ugly face, she tried to break it off. He let her know in no uncertain terms she was his until he decided to end it."

His hand tightened on the phone. "What did he do to her?"

The long pause made his stomach roil. "That's for her to tell."

"Tara, she won't talk to me. I frighten her. Why don't you just tell me why?"

After a long pause, she sighed. "He held her down, beat her, might have done more, but she kneed him. Girl's got gumption."

"Fucking bastard."

"Yeah, exactly. She filed a report. As soon as the cops heard the name of her assailant, DEA was all over her, wanting her to testify to add another nail to his coffin."

"What can I do for her the cops aren't able to do?"

"Care about her. Keep an eye out. They seem more eager to capture him than keep her safe."

He didn't like having his suspicions confirmed. "She thought they were using her as bait."

"Well, now you know why she needs you."

Mac raked his hand through his hair. "Still think you got the wrong guy. I'm a fucking cripple."

Her low, easy laughter confirmed another thing—she'd chosen him deliberately. "You're balls to the wall, McDonough. Doesn't matter if you have to crawl to gnaw on the bastard's shin bones, you won't let him get her."

"Anyone ever tell you you're manipulative as fuck?"

"Played you well, didn't I? Still feeling horny?"

Mac snorted, not knowing whether to laugh or groan. "Yeah, but looks like that brand of comfort is the last thing she needs."

"She's stronger than you think. And she's never had one of the good guys taking care of her."

"Do me a favor: cut the matchmaking crap. I'm here. I'll keep her safe."

"Get some rest yourself."

"You made sure that was impossible," he growled.

More low, sexy laughter stirred his cock.

Mac waited for her to grow quiet. "We're gonna need supplies if we're here a while."

"I'll take care of it. You take care of yourself, soldier boy."

Mac closed the phone and stared into the darkness. The thickness of his semi-aroused cock appeared to be a permanent affliction. One he'd have to suffer over the next few days because he wasn't going anywhere. Whether he liked it or not, one set of wide brown eyes had pulled him right out of the land of the almost dead.

When rain began pinging against the tin roof of the cabin, weariness dragged at his eyelids. Used to sleeping in catnaps anyway, he didn't worry he wouldn't wake up at the slightest creak of the floorboards.

With the picture still in his head of Suki standing in the kitchen with her white-knuckled grip caressing the trigger, he closed his eyes.

3

Mac jerked awake, not sure what had disturbed him. Rain still fell against the roof in a steady, soothing shower—the likely reason he'd slept so heavily. He pressed the button at the side of his watch and read the time on the illuminated dial. Only a couple of hours had passed.

Time to make another round and check doors and windows. Just to be on the safe side.

He grunted as he swung his leg off the sofa and stood, cautiously adding weight. The piercing ache had diminished, but stiffness remained. He grabbed his cane and hobbled to the front door and then flicked off the porch light before stepping outside.

As he stood in the darkness, he lit a cigarette, cupping his palm around the end to hide the embers, a habit he'd picked up during his mobilization. He dragged nicotine into his lungs until the jagged edges of his hunger smoothed to a civilized scrape.

Then he returned to the house and walked quietly through the rooms, checking windows and closets. At Suki's bedroom door, he halted.

Muffled murmurs came from inside. All in her voice. Was she talking in her sleep? Or using a cell phone? While the first possibility bothered him, the second couldn't be ignored.

He tried the door handle and discovered it was locked. Against him. Smart girl.

He tapped softly. "Suki, are you awake?"

The murmurs stopped. Dead silence echoed beyond the door.

"It's me, Mac. Are you all right?"

The door opened, and her pale face appeared in the crack. "Did you need something?" she asked, her voice husky after being pulled from her bed.

Not something you ask a horny man. Mac gave her a crooked smile. "Just checking doors and windows. I heard noises in here."

A yawn stretched her mouth. "I was dreaming."

"So you're getting some sleep?"

She nodded sleepily, a smile softening her mouth. "Didn't think I would."

"Good," he said curtly, thinking he'd better get out of the doorway quick. The smell of her sleep-warmed skin was driving him crazy.

"What about you?" she asked, leaning against edge of the door. "Did you sleep?"

He shrugged. "Guess I better let you get back to bed."

Her gaze lifted shyly to his. "Mac?"

His fingers wrapped around the door frame. There was something about the way she looked at him, drowsy eyed, her skin flushed, that made him wish he could follow her inside the bedroom. Just to slide between the sheets and hold her.

"I'm sorry I was so bitchy before. Guess I was so tired I couldn't think straight. Everyone looks like the bad guy."

"Not a problem. I didn't behave my best either." He cleared his throat. "This is where I'll say good night, but I'd prefer it if you didn't lock the door. Just in case I need to get in here in a hurry."

She gave him a vague nod. "Thing is," she said softly, "it's too quiet, and there's only this one bed. I think maybe I'll sleep better if you're here."

Mac froze. His cock, however, stirred, beginning to warm and fill. "Get under the sheets. I'll stretch out on top of the blankets."

She opened the door wider, and he saw she wore only a tank top and bikini panties. Probably too tired to remember she was only half dressed.

Suki stumbled to the bed, placed the shotgun on the floor beside it, and then crawled onto the mattress, giving him a mind-blowing view of her pretty, heart-shaped bottom and slim legs.

Mac sucked in a deep breath, a rueful grin curving his lips. God had a wicked sense of humor. He finally had a woman in a bed, but he couldn't touch her.

He stood his cane beside the door and walked around to the far side of the bed. With his back to her, he sat on the edge and pulled off his boots and socks and then stripped his belt from his loops. That was as far as he dared go.

Lying down beside her, he stuck his hands under his head and stared at the ceiling.

She lay on her side, facing him. "How'd you hurt your leg?" she asked quietly.

Mac slowly inhaled. He hadn't liked talking about it before, but something about the quiet room with the rain pattering on the roof over his head kept the anger at bay. "My unit was making a sweep of a neighborhood, looking for insurgents. We were on foot patrol. I was on point . . . at the front of the formation. It was getting dark, and we'd been at it for a while. We were all hot, dirty, and sweaty . . . ready to meet up with the trucks and convoy back to our barracks."

He drew a deep breath and continued as unemotionally as he could manage. "Just one last street to go. I saw a grocery bag. A white, plastic grocery bag lying in the gutter, the ties fluttering in the breeze. It caught my eye. The breeze didn't move the bag. Something told me it wasn't right. I held up my hand to give the signal to halt but didn't get a chance to do any more than that when it exploded. It was an IED. Guess whoever was watching figured he wasn't gonna get a better target and set it off."

Mac may have stared at the dark ceiling, but memories rolled past in quick, painful bursts. "All hell broke loose, but I hardly noticed. My leg burned like it was on fire. My guys were all around me, shouting into the radio. I don't remember much after that. Don't remember them getting me to medevac or the trip to Germany. I woke up in Walter Reed after surgery." He turned his head toward her. "That's it."

"You say that so calmly."

His lips curved ruefully. "I've had months to get used to it."

"Anyone else hit?"

"Thank God, no."

"Does it hurt much?"

He nodded and turned to stare at the ceiling again, not wanting to read sympathy in her steady gaze. "But it gets better every day," he said, realizing it was true. A month ago a walk through the woods wouldn't have been possible.

"I'm glad you're here."

Mac smiled and reached across the mattress, enfolding her hand in his. "Me, too. You should go to sleep."

Her breaths evened almost immediately.

Mac pulled her hand over his belly, laced his fingers with hers, and resigned himself to the fact he wouldn't get another wink of sleep for the rest of the night.

No way would he let anything disturb her dreams.

Being this close was just enough to fill his senses with *woman*. Pulling in her scent with every breath, listening to the sound of her soft, sighing exhalations—sure, he was harder than a fence post, but he'd never felt more like a man. She needed him.

When Suki snuggled closer and rested her head on his shoulder, he felt as though he'd been given a gift. Her thick hair tickled his nose and fanned around the corner of his shoulder. Such a little thing. Not a sexual move in the least, but still his body hardened further.

When her breath feathered the side of his neck, he gritted his teeth.

He was in for one helluva long night.

Suki became aware of water falling. At first, she thought it was the rain, but the sound was closer.

The shower was running.

She reached across the bed and confirmed she was alone. Mac, her surly protector, must be taking a shower.

Feeling rested for the first time in weeks, she stretched, enjoying the quiet sounds. Enjoying the scent of him permeating her sheets. Soap, a light tang of tobacco, his own brand of masculine musk.

So intimate. His scent, his sounds. A man in her shower. A man she'd shared a bed with. One who hadn't done more than offer his company so she could feel safe while she slept.

Not wanting to dwell on the warmth that filled her at the thought, Suki decided the least she could do was offer him a home-cooked breakfast. She tossed back the sheets, climbed out of bed, and began to dress.

In the hallway, she paused outside the bathroom. The door was cracked open. She remembered his admonition about not locking doors against him and guessed it went both ways.

The temptation to peek inside was overwhelming. Her hand touched the door, and then she quickly pulled back. What was she thinking?

Then she heard the unmistakable sounds. Like wet slaps, increasing in speed. Suki pressed her lips together, trying not to smile.

Was this his morning routine, or had he been inspired?

She hurried down the hallway, giving him privacy.

As she pulled out pans and ingredients and began to cook, she couldn't help thinking about him and what he'd told her last night. Fresh from the Middle East and treatment in a hospital, was she the first woman he'd been alone with?

The thought left her feeling guilty about teasing him, however innocent her intentions, leaving him without any recourse but to relieve himself alone in the shower.

Still, regret didn't explain the excitement that thrummed throughout her body, pricking at her nipples and lending a slight tremor to her hands.

What kind of deviant was she anyway? Running from one abusive man and then lusting after another Cro-Magnon archetype? And why did she still feel an overwhelming urge to slip into the bathroom and see what Mac McDonough had to offer?

"Good morning."

The egg she'd raised came slamming down on the edge of the bowl, the shell collapsing and instantly scrambling the yolk that spilled onto the countertop.

"Didn't mean to startle you," Mac said, reaching around her

for a paper towel. With his arm enclosing her, and his belly near enough to warm her back, she grew stiff.

"Fuck." Mac stepped away immediately. "Didn't mean to crowd you."

Suki knew he thought she'd freaked at being close to a man. "Are you going to be apologizing for the rest of the day?" She glanced over her shoulder with a wry grin. "You don't have to walk on eggshells around me."

Mac's eyes blinked, and then a slow, sexy grin curved his lips. "Unless you're doing the cooking, hmmm?"

She smiled in apology. "I was deep in thought when you came in. Anyone would have made me jump out of my skin."

"Sure," he said, though his expression remained doubtful.

"I'm not afraid of you. I swear it."

"Well, that's progress."

From the corner of her eye, her gaze swept his body. Another T-shirt, this time blue, and faded jeans hugged his formidable torso and thighs. His bare feet peeked from beneath the bottom edges.

Suki swallowed at the strong pull of Mac's sensual appeal. "Plates are in the cupboard," she said, lifting her spatula to point at the cabinet beside her.

Again he approached, careful this time not to touch.

Oddly disappointed, she slid eggs onto the plates and bent to pull a plate of bacon from the warming tray in the oven.

When she straightened, his glance slid quickly back to her face.

Suki couldn't help her lop-sided smile and decided not to pretend to ignore his interest. "Were you checking out my ass?"

Mac snorted. "Guess I'll be apologizing all day long."

She walked to the table and slid the dish to the center beside a basket of biscuits. "I really didn't mind," she murmured.

Mac held out a chair for her and then took his own, quickly

lifting his fork and changing the subject. "Anyone we need to check in with today?"

"Let's not talk about it. The rain stopped. It looks like it's going to be a nice day."

His nod said he was ready to follow her lead. "Too bad we don't have a boat. We could go fishing."

"You like to fish?"

"Haven't been in a long time, but all that water right outside the door . . . It's tempting."

Suki stuck her fork into her eggs and pushed them around her plate. "Maybe we could go for a swim," she said, her voice a little breathless.

He chewed slowly, his expression growing alert. "I didn't bring a suit."

She swallowed to wet her dry mouth. "Neither did I."

"Not a problem for me. I can wear my boxers."

The evenness of his voice didn't tell her whether he was getting the hint or not. She decided to go for blunt. "Why bother with anything? It's just you and me."

"Suki . . ." A deep breath expanded his chest. "I haven't been alone with a woman in a long time. I'm not sure I can go skinny-dipping without embarrassing myself."

Suki bit her lip to keep from smiling. "Somehow I don't think you'll have a thing to be embarrassed about."

Mac lifted a forkful of eggs to his mouth, his gaze narrowing on her face.

She met his gaze, and, miraculously, her cheeks didn't heat with a single blush. She smiled and bit into a piece of crisp bacon. Maybe Mac was just the antidote she needed for the tension that had gripped her for weeks.

"Just so you know," he said, seeming to struggle with words, "I don't expect anything to happen . . . between us."

"Why don't we just have a good time? No expectations."

His nod was slow, but already she detected subtle changes as arousal gripped him. His jaw tightened. His narrowed gaze flickered over her. He shifted in his seat and attacked his breakfast as though he thought he might need sustenance.

Suki suppressed a smile and ate slowly, enjoying the sensual awareness warming her own body. Enjoying the power she seemed to wield over such a dark and dangerous man.

Power he ceded easily, as though it was natural for him to let her take the lead. Perhaps he'd sensed she needed that to soothe her fears. Or maybe, at his core, he truly was a gentle man despite his appearance and gruff manners.

Whichever the case, her appreciation for him grew, as did her desire.

When she'd finally finished, Suki gathered their plates and set them in the sink. "Why don't you find us some towels?"

Knowing he would have to head to the bathroom again, she rushed to the bedroom and pulled open the top drawer of the nightstand, gathering several foil packets and cramming them into her jeans pocket.

When she heard his feet padding down the hall, she met him at the door.

After his polite nod for her to proceed, she sauntered down the corridor, Mac on her heels.

Out the door, down the path through the woods, the scent of wet vegetation and pure, fresh air lightened her mood and her steps, which she kept slow so he didn't have to fight to keep up. With excitement escalating her heartbeats, the walk to the end of the pier seemed endless.

At the covered end of the dock, he tossed the towels onto the plank floor and stood with his hands on his hips, his gaze cutting across the lake and then around the woods that edged the water.

While he checked the area for bad guys, she took her

courage into her hands and thumbed open the button at the top of her jeans and then pushed them down her legs. However bold that move had been, she turned away to slip off her tank top, nervous about having him find her a little "less" than he might prefer.

Standing in her underwear, she gave him a glance over her shoulder, satisfied she had his attention, and then reached behind her to unclip her bra.

As the small cups fell away, she took a deep breath, gathering her courage around her, and turned. Slowly she slid down the straps, holding the garment over the growing pile of her clothing, inviting him to examine her.

His gaze held hers for only a moment and then slid over her breasts. Air hissed softly between his teeth.

When she dropped the bra beside her feet, she reached quickly for the thin straps at each side of her hips and pulled down the silky underwear.

She straightened and found it hard to suck in a deep breath, a little shocked at her own behavior. Had she really just shucked all her clothing in front of a man she'd met only yesterday?

The urge had come so fast, so strong, she hadn't paused even once to question where it had come from.

His expression growing more taut and dangerous by the second, he appeared every bit as desperate as she felt.

"Do you need any help?" she asked softly.

"I can manage," he growled in a voice that matched the fierce, predatory expression darkening his face.

"I mean, I know you don't bend very well," she said, licking her lips nervously. "I could manage your pants."

"That's kind of you," he bit out, "but I've been undressing myself for weeks now." His head canted to the side. "That is . . . unless you really want to?"

4

Suki managed a rueful smile. "Did I look disappointed?"

"Like I just stole your candy," he drawled.

They shared smiles, and Suki relaxed and stepped closer. Her hands pushed up his T-shirt, but he was so tall he had to take over to get it past his shoulders and head.

As he bared his abdomen and chest, Suki's breaths shortened. Hard and tanned as polished oak, his body had her reaching out to follow the swells of his defined musculature, gliding over skin as smooth as oiled leather. Crisp, brown curls stretched between his flat nipples, arrowing down his belly to disappear into his jeans.

Looking down, her gaze snagged on the fullness swelling inside his jeans. She licked her lips again and raised her glance, finding his green eyes glittering, his nostrils flaring. The feral hunger tightening his features filled her with elation.

She opened his pants, dragging down his zipper, all the while holding his gaze until she reached the bottom.

"Better let me take care of the rest," he ground out.

Instead of conceding, she could scarcely believe her own temerity. She slid her hand inside his snug pants and cupped his thick erection.

His cock heated her palm, expanding as she gently squeezed.

"Seems a waste," she whispered.

"What does?"

"The water's going to be cool."

His eyes narrowed. "Ahhh . . . maybe I should just ease into it now."

She bit her lower lip to trap the grin tugging her mouth wide. "Let me help you with this." She knelt on one knee and pulled down his pants, eager now to see what she'd held inside her hand.

She pushed the pants all the way down, forcing her gaze to follow. The white, zipperlike scars of his incisions and shallow circles dotting his leg lay in stark contrast against his deeply tanned skin.

Afraid to touch them unless she caused him pain, she waited while he stepped out of his jeans. Only then did she raise her face level with his cock.

The proud, straight thrust of him made her mouth water.

She spared a glance at his tense face, noting the lean hunger sharpening his features to a razor's edge.

Then, closing her eyes, she rubbed her cheek along his length, savoring the satiny feel of the skin that stretched around his shaft, dragging in the scent of his natural musk.

Her hands came up between his legs, smoothing over the sparse hairs on his inner thighs, rising steadily until she turned her palms to cup his balls.

They filled her small palms, and she closed her fingers around them, tugging gently.

Mac's fingers wrapped around the back of her head, not

guiding, not pressuring her to do more than she wanted—just lightly caressing her scalp, threading through her hair as she worked up the courage to take him.

Her mouth opened, and she skimmed her lips along his shaft until she reached the curved ridge at the underside of the crown. Turning her head sideways, she stuck out her tongue and licked beneath his glans, opening her eyes to check his reaction and finding his gaze boring into hers. She stroked him again with her tongue.

His chest lifted on a ragged inhalation. His cock rocked forward, gliding along her lips.

She wrapped the fingers of both hands around his shaft, capturing him with a firm grasp, and pulled his cock toward her mouth, rounding her lips to take just the cap inside her mouth. She suctioned against the soft skin, swirling her tongue over it, sinking the tip of her tongue into the narrow slit and then fluttering inside it until Mac's hands tugged her hair harder to urge her closer.

She opened her jaws, taking a little more of his length inside. Then she shielded her teeth with her lips to gobble at the crown as she drew off.

"*Sweet . . . fuck!*" He pulled one of his hands from her hair and moved hers from his shaft, grasping himself just below the crown.

Then, pointing himself straight between her lips, he painted her mouth with the moisture she'd left behind as she pursed her lips to accept his "kiss."

Watching him while he watched her lips got her hot as hell. Color glazed his cheeks while his lips peeled away from his teeth. He looked like a man on the verge of getting every dream come true.

He punched his cock gently between her lips, forcing her to take exactly as much as he desired.

As he gave her more of his cock, he eased his hand back, his fingers acting as a guard, preventing her from taking more.

Which she was surprisingly greedy and eager to do. Suki glided her hands over his hips, reaching around him to clasp his hard ass and give her better balance as she began to bob her head forward and back. Her breaths deepened as she herself grew more aroused.

But he controlled the depth of her pulses, and suddenly Suki wanted to push him past control.

At the end of her forward pulse, she drew hard, suctioning as she came off him, and then releasing as he sank inside her mouth again.

"*Jesus!* Again," he groaned.

If she hadn't been so aroused, she might have smiled at the edge of desperation straining his voice.

She bobbed deeper, sucking him as she drew backward, repeating the motions—suctioning, releasing, suctioning—until his thick thighs trembled against her and his breaths grew jagged.

When her jaws began to ache, she came off him and leaned her head against his thigh while she gasped for breath.

His fingers curled around her head, urging her upward.

Her legs wobbled as she rose, and she reached for his broad shoulders to steady herself.

His hands clamped around her waist and lifted her high so her breasts were even with his mouth. As his lips closed around one turgid peak, her head fell back, and she moaned.

Her fingers slid through his short hair as he suckled one breast and then the other, and then he shifted and bit out a curse.

His leg. "Should you be holding me up?" she moaned as he tongued her nipple.

He turned his head, breathing hard against her skin. "We need protection."

"In my pocket," she said, sliding her arms around his shoulders.

His mouth rooted against her breast again, his tongue swirling on the tip, and then he lowered her to her feet.

Suki knelt quickly, her hands shaking as she turned her pocket inside out and plucked up one of the foil packets that spilled onto the wood deck. She tore it open and held it up to him, knowing her hands shook too badly to apply it.

Blowing out a deep breath, he cupped the rubber and curved his hand around the crown of his cock and rolled it down his length.

The latex stretched around his girth, becoming transparent as the rubber stretched to its limits. As soon as he had it in place, she rose in front of him, not sure how she wanted him to take her, not sure what he could manage with his damaged leg.

His glance cut from her to the end of the pier and the peaked roof of the covering. "Get inside," he bit out.

She walked unsteadily toward the covered end, with him following close behind.

Mac followed Suki, his gaze glued to the sway of her slim hips, still not believing how quickly things had progressed between them.

Before stepping beneath the covering, he cut a quick glance around the water's edge.

This was a bad idea. But the urgent heat building in his body was a distraction. One he had to ease before he could get his mind wrapped around what he needed to do.

He'd take her quickly, get them both off in minutes, and then sit at the edge of the pier while she swam and he kept watch.

Suki stood beneath the peaked, shingled roof. The sides were open, but long planks, which served as part of the frame, stretched the length of both sides.

Mac noted her tension and wondered if she might be having second thoughts. Her hands curled tightly at her sides. "We don't have to do this, you know. You've already given me more pleasure than I had the right to expect."

"I'm not hesitating . . . not really," she said, her breaths coming fast. "I'm just . . . tense. So excited, I can hardly breathe."

He closed the distance between them and lifted his hands to frame her small face. Bending low, he swept his mouth over hers once, brushing her with a tentative kiss.

Her soft sigh drifted across his lips, and a deep, rumbling growl broke from between his. "I'm afraid I'm gonna get a little rough."

One corner of her mouth quirked up. "Having trouble holding it together?"

"Uh-huh."

"You're tall. Will I be high enough here if I bend over?"

She was too damn short for that to work. Mac closed his eyes. A year ago, he would just have lifted her in his arms and slid her body down until she engulfed him. "The water. Let's do it in the water."

She nodded quickly. "Yeah, I won't be as heavy. Will the temperature be a problem?"

They talked as calmly as if he didn't have a raging hard-on and her thighs weren't slippery with her cream. "Nothin's gonna wilt me now."

She turned and took two steps toward the end of the covered pier and dove into the water, surfacing several feet away.

With her hair slicked back, she looked very small, very young. Completely edible to a hungry "grunt."

Not nearly as agile, he walked toward the edge and lowered

himself carefully to sit with his legs dangling over the side. Then he pushed off, and water closed over his head.

When he came up for air, he found her treading water beside him, her eyes gleaming with excitement. "It's not too deep just around the side. Follow me."

Anywhere you want, kitten. You've got the catnip.

Around the side of the pier, she paused and then sank below the water before bouncing back up. "Should be just about right here."

Mac treaded closer and let his legs drift to the bottom. He planted his feet in soft sand and stood. "Not bad. I'm surprised the doctors didn't recommend this for therapy."

Her grin stretched, and she swam closer and reached for his shoulders. "This work for you?"

He nodded, afraid he'd sound like a caveman with all her soft "parts" snuggling closer to his. He placed his hands gently around her waist and brought her flush against his body. "We should have done this in a bed. I would have given you as much attention as you gave to me."

With her wet lashes sticking together like points of a star, she searched his gaze. "Don't worry about me not being ready for this. I have the feeling I'm going to go off like a rocket as soon as you slide up inside me."

"You're built kinda tiny," he said gruffly.

She leaned close and nipped his chin with her teeth. "Might take a little wiggling to get you all the way up," she whispered, "but I sure want to try it."

"You shouldn't say things like that to a man."

"Am I being too slutty?"

"*Fuck no.* Soon as you said it, though, my dick got harder just imagining it."

"Afraid you're gonna pop right through that latex?"

"It's a little snug."

One dark eyebrow arched. "I noticed."

Mac's hands roamed over her smooth back, sliding lower over the slight curves of her buttocks. His fingers tightened. "Wrap your legs around my waist."

Her arms tightened around his shoulders, and she drifted closer, slowly winding her legs over the tops of his hips. "Sure this isn't hurting you?"

"It's all good," he breathed, his cock sliding under her open sex. "Can you reach between us? Guide me inside?"

As one arm tightened around his neck, her hand snuck between them, smoothing down his belly, which tensed and rippled as she passed.

Suki's growing smile said she knew exactly what she was about. Her fingers spread, spearing through the hair at his groin to tug, and then bypassed his cock altogether to heft his balls in her palm.

"Feeling a little chilled?" she drawled.

Mac shook his head. "You know you're playing with fire, here?" he asked, his voice rasping like sandpaper.

"Are you nearly at the end of your tether?"

"You'll find out if you don't wrap your hand around my dick fast."

Her lips pursed. "Ooh! I love it when a man talks dirty."

"Is that what I've been doing wrong?"

"You haven't made a single misstep where I'm concerned." Her smile slid away. "I didn't want to feel this way, you know?"

Mac fought the urge to take control and ram deep inside her. Instead he rested his forehead against hers. "What way is that?"

With her lips just beneath his, she whispered. "Hot, trembling inside. I want this just as bad as you do."

"Then why are you playing games now?"

"I don't know. Maybe I want to see you when you're pushed past politeness."

Mac couldn't resist the invitation of that natural pout and pressed a kiss to her lush lips. "I don't want to scare you."

"I think I need a little shaking up. 'Sides, fucking in a lake isn't exactly scary."

He raised one eyebrow. "Haven't had me comin' up inside you yet, have you? If the condom I have squeezing my dick is any indication of what you're used to, I might be a little too much for you to handle."

Her hand released his balls and closed around him. He gently raised her bottom, and she slid his cock between her legs, pushing the tip against her folds.

"Water's not going to be as good a lubricant," he groaned, rutting to push the head into her entrance and then lifting her hips up and down to force himself deeper inside her. "Not as slick, not as warm."

"I don't care. I don't want it easy."

Mac watched her face as he shoved her down his cock.

Her full upper lip pushed outward as she slowly blew out a deep breath. Her nostrils flared. Her eyes blinked and then slid halfway closed as he tunneled deeper inside her.

Her cunt clasped around his cock in a tight grip that eased as he began to pump her hips, sliding her up and down his shaft, sinking her deeper with each downward thrust.

"Oh, Mac!" she breathed, leaning back to change the angle of the strokes. Her fingernails bit into his shoulders.

Mac couldn't push words past his tight throat to reassure her. His arms began to burn as he thrust her harder, up and down, faster and faster, working her tight cunt gradually down his dick until she swallowed all of him.

At the end of one long stroke, he ground the base of his cock against the top of her folds, trying to excite her clit, wanting her to come apart before he exploded.

His whole body felt tight, muscles tense and burning.

Suki's breaths rasped, low, guttural moans breaking past her lips as he quickened the strokes.

Her eyes squeezed shut, and her head fell back; Her body slackened in his embrace. "God, oh, God!" she chanted. Then her back arched suddenly, and her thighs clutched him close.

Mac gripped her ass harder and shoved her up and down in shallow, grinding thrusts, churning the water trapped between them until, at last, a thin, keening cry ripped from her throat.

Her fingers slid down his chest and trailed into the water. Her tight, straining features relaxed while her shuddering breaths shook her tiny breasts.

Mac let go of her ass and hugged her close, holding her tight until her arms came around him and she bent her head to rest it against his shoulder.

As her breaths evened, he detected a soft, ragged edge of a sob, and his belly tensed. "It's okay, Suki. It's okay, baby."

Her face nuzzled the corner of his neck, and she hugged him. Then she sniffed and raised her head. The smile trembling on her lips twisted. "I promise I don't get weepy every time I climax. You were right. You . . . It was a bit much."

"We should get you back to the cabin," he said quietly, though, inside, he wanted to howl with frustration.

"But what about you?"

"I'll take care of it."

She shook her head. "No way."

"We've been out here a while. It's not safe in the open."

"Come back to the cabin with me. I'll finish it. I promise."

Mac hugged her close, pressing her face against his shoulder. "Maybe later. Right now, I need you to get dressed, okay?"

Her nod was slow in coming, but she unwound her legs, gave him a look filled with regret, and then swam to the pier and climbed easily over the edge.

Mac followed more slowly, embarrassed with how difficult

it was to maneuver his body out of the water. He had the strength to pull himself up, got his good knee over, but struggled not to bump his leg too badly.

To top it all off, getting vertical proved another trial.

By the time he got to his feet, she was walking toward him, fully dressed, his clothing clutched in her arms.

"Get back to the house," he said, damning himself to hell when her expression fell.

"I'll hel—"

"I'll manage on my own," he ground out more harshly than he'd intended, but after all the time in the water, his weak leg trembled, and he didn't want her to notice.

She passed the clothing to his hands and walked away, not looking back even once.

Mac sighed. He'd wanted a willing woman but not one he actually might want to see again. Definitely not someone he was starting to care about.

By the time he'd wrestled his body back into his clothing, he'd found what was left of his sense of humor. Stuffing his cock behind the metal zipper, he caught himself cussing and started to chuckle. He'd had high hopes a short while ago that this particular problem would be solved.

Considering his luck lately, he was fortunate he hadn't scraped it raw hauling himself over the deck.

But his losing streak was doomed to bite him in the ass one last time.

As he entered the clearing, he spotted a black pickup, and the cursing started again.

5

When he pushed open the door, he found Lyssa and Brand sitting across from Suki, whose expression seemed relieved when he entered.

Lyssa sprang from the sofa and rushed over to Mac, giving him a hug he couldn't stop himself from returning. He closed his eyes as he held his sister close. The last time he'd seen her, he'd shouted her out of his hospital room.

"You look amazing," she said, her voice thick with tears as she leaned back inside his embrace.

"You look . . . happy," he returned with a crooked smile.

Brand cleared his throat. The glance Brand shot him said he wasn't feelin' the love. Probably still held a grudge for how badly Mac had treated Lyssa.

Mac lifted his chin. "Brand."

Brand didn't reply, but his eyes narrowed as he raised a hand along the back of the sofa, as though he intended to stay a while.

Mac was more than ready to disabuse him of that thought.

"Mac," Lyssa said, drawing his attention away from her grumpy boyfriend, "we were just extending an invitation to Suki to come back to the ranch with us."

Mac stiffened. What they proposed made sense. She'd be safer there, surrounded by acres of private property and staff.

"I appreciate it," Suki said quickly, sounding a little panicked, "but I'm doing just fine here. Of course, I understand if you need to head home, Mac."

Anger swept through him, leaving a bitter taste in his mouth. Did she have to get snippy just because he'd cut their tryst a little short? He'd been right, after all: Brand and Lyssa might have walked right up on them when they were still going at it in the water.

"As long as you decide to hole up here," he said, keeping his voice even, "I'm staying. So get that thought out of your head now."

Her eyes widened innocently. "I wasn't trying to push you out the door."

"Sure you weren't," he said. "But there's no way in hell I'm leaving you here alone."

Her eyes narrowed just a fraction. "Yesterday you were just fine with a 'flyby.' "

"*Yesterday* I didn't fully understand the danger you're flirting with here."

Suki's chin came up.

Brand coughed behind his hand, no doubt to hide a smile.

Mac aimed a deadly glare his way.

Lyssa's curious gaze trailed over Suki's damp hair and Mac's T-shirt, which still clung to his wet skin. When her eyes rose to meet his gaze, they gleamed with wicked humor. "Brought you some clothes, though doesn't look like you'll have much need for them."

"Lyssa . . ."

"I'm not judging."

He narrowed his gaze in warning. "You're in no position to pass judgment."

"Exactly," she said, a blush beginning to bloom on her cheeks. She took a deep breath and raised her eyebrows high. "I suppose we'd be overextending our welcome if we stayed for dinner?"

Mac gave her a thin-lipped smile. "Wouldn't want you on the road past dark."

Lyssa leaned close for another hug. "She's cute," she whispered in his ear. "Tiny thing, but doesn't look like a pushover."

"She can stand up for herself."

"Tara said sparks were flyin'."

"You tell Tara I'll spank her ass good if she meddles again."

Lyssa blushed clear to her roots and backed up quick. "Brand?" she said in a squeaky voice.

Brand reached over to shake Suki's hand. "Don't get up. We'll let ourselves out."

After their footsteps faded, Mac walked slowly to the vacated sofa and sank against the cushions. "So you met the family. They're a bit overwhelming."

"You're lucky." He lifted an eyebrow in question. "They love you."

He snorted. "Guess that's what that was all about."

"What else would it be?"

"Them coming over to check you out."

Her eyes widened. "How would they know?"

"Tara's been matchmaking. Something she can't resist when her own love life's in the shitter. Pardon my French."

Suki smiled. "Think they knew?"

Mac snorted. "Oh, yeah."

"What gave it away?"

"Besides the fact we're both soaking wet? And your lips are a little swollen?"

Her hand shot up to her mouth, and fingers slid across her lips. "Anything else?" she murmured.

"My pleasant disposition."

Her eyebrows rose. "Or, more the point, your lack of . . . ?"

"Yeah."

"Great," she huffed. "They think they interrupted something."

He opened his mouth to deliver another biting comment and then realized he'd been enjoying their exchange a little too much. "I'm hitting the shower."

She pulled her bottom lip between her teeth and nodded.

Schooling his face not to wince when he swung his leg off the couch, he stood and walked carefully to the bathroom.

Once inside, he stripped, turned the water to a scalding temperature, and braced his hands on either side of the narrow stall as water sluiced down his front.

The stall door clicked, and he glanced behind him.

Suki stood in the opening. "I figured 'shower' was just another word for 'jerking off,' " she said, her chin lifting high.

Glancing down at his cock, he could hardly deny that had been his intent. "I'll be just a minute."

When he sensed her still hovering behind him, he gave her a wry, regretful smile. "Go get dressed. I need to have a look around your place again. No time for fun and games now."

"I'm more than willing. Fair's fair."

He aimed a baleful glare her way. "I wasn't giving you anything because I expected it to be returned."

"I don't get you, Mac McDonough."

Her large brown eyes gave him a look that reminded him of a wounded puppy dog. Damn, he didn't want to care that he kept hurting her. "I know you don't. And it's a damn shame you've been conditioned to expect a man to act that way. I want you. I won't deny that. But your safety and well being come first. I let myself forget that for a little while."

"I'll leave you alone," she said, stepping back and closing the stall door.

Mac hung his head beneath the spray and took deep breaths. He'd been seconds from pulling her inside, pushing her to her knees, and forcing his cock between her soft lips.

But the next time he had her naked, he wanted to love her without restriction. Without having to think about his goddamn leg or whether it was safe to let down his guard and just enjoy being inside her.

In the meantime, he didn't need any distractions. He reached down, wrapped his hand around himself and pretended he rocked between a set of lush, swollen lips.

Suki sat in the living room while evening shadows slowly filled the spaces around her.

Mac had been busy most of the afternoon, hammer in hand, repairing latches that might be jimmied by an intruder. He'd roamed the house like a caged bear, his uneven steps stomping through the house as he checked doors, closets, and windows time and again.

Moments ago, he'd left to trek down the road toward the highway after hearing an engine slow in the distance.

She was beginning to think he was avoiding her.

All right, she knew damn well that was precisely his strategy. Ever since he'd chased his sister and her boyfriend out the door, he'd been surly, his already dour expression turning to stone.

If she hadn't known for a certainty he still desired her, she'd have thought that maybe the sex they shared had been awful.

However, his constant state of arousal was impossible to miss. Even if she hadn't noticed that his grouchiness seemed to sharpen every time his gaze lingered on her, the knot at the front of his trousers was a dead giveaway.

As large as he was, erections weren't something Mac could easily hide.

So while he slammed around the house, Suki had played it cool, fighting a devious smile each time he left the room in a huff to find something else to keep him far away from her.

Funny how, just yesterday, she'd been fearful and tense, but today she'd found something wonderfully delicious to fill her thoughts. She was truly grateful Mac had entered her life, but would he still be interested when the danger passed? It seemed he had his own demons to conquer and a torn body to heal.

Voices sifted through the windows, speaking softly. One belonged to Mac. From his even tone, she guessed the law had arrived.

Suki wandered out onto the porch and waited as Mac led a uniformed sheriff's deputy down the path.

"Howdy, ma'am," the officer said, his sharp glance taking in her relaxed pose. "I was just telling Mac here that we'll be stopping to check on you."

She reached out to take the hand he offered, mumbled a greeting, and shifted closer to Mac.

Mac's arm wrapped around her shoulder, and he brought her close. "We're taking precautions. But we do appreciate your keeping an eye out for us."

The officer handed her a card. "Nine-one-one will bring us quick, but you can reach me at this number, too. You two stay safe." He touched the brim of his cream cowboy hat and left.

Mac turned Suki in his arms. "The deputy's concerned. There are too many ways for a man to get to this house, and from too many directions. It's just not smart to stay here, Suki.

Maybe you should rethink. My ranch would be safer and not a place your old boyfriend is familiar with."

She snuggled closer in his embrace, happy that he wasn't trying to shunt her back to some safe house and seemed to want her to stay with him. "All right. If that's what you want." She lifted her head. "But can we leave tomorrow?"

At his terse nod, she sighed. She had just one more night alone with Mac. But would he be as standoffish as he'd been all afternoon when it came time to go to bed?

Mac made a final check and then padded barefoot back to the living room. He eyed the sofa with its lumpy cushions and grimaced.

Who was he fooling? He had no intention of bedding down here when Suki had made it very apparent she didn't mind sharing with him again.

Tomorrow they'd be at the ranch, surrounded by family and hands. Would she be as amenable to sharing a bed when everyone in the house would know exactly where she slept?

He didn't think she was a prude, but maybe he was . . . just a little bit. He'd never brought a woman home. Somehow the thought of sleeping under his own roof, with his sister down the hall, made it seem like a declaration of sorts. It wouldn't just be sex with a willing woman, but sex with a woman who mattered to him.

Mac shrugged off the thoughts. He was a grown man with needs. Lyss could go to hell if she started making wedding plans before he'd even decided whether he liked the woman, much less loved her enough to marry her.

Though, he liked everything he'd learned so far. In fact, he craved another look at her slender body. Not that sex was the only thing that attracted him—he liked the hints of humor

212

she'd betrayed as he'd slammed through the house today, trying to keep busy so he wasn't tempted to "get busier" with her.

Her lips had pressed together as though she'd suppressed a smile every time he'd aimed an annoyed glance her way. She didn't buy his attitude.

Must have been the hard-on he couldn't outrun.

His hand crept between his legs, and he cupped himself and then adjusted his cock, letting it rise against his belly. He'd caught her curious gaze checking him out more times than he could count, and still she hadn't said a word. Or, when she did, it was something so ordinary he'd catch himself staring at her as if she'd lost her mind.

And then he'd note the amusement gleaming in her eyes.

Suki was subtle. And stubborn.

And she was winning the battle through a careful strategy of attrition.

She'd conserved her energy, worn him out by keeping him on the move until he was ready to knock on her bedroom door and wave a white flag.

All the doors had been checked; he'd circled the house twice, walked to the end of the pier, and had listened for sounds of approaching boats. Nothing.

He could bed down, could bed down with her. So what was really stopping him?

"Mac . . . ?"

Stifling a groan, he tore his glance from the window overlooking the porch to find her standing behind him wearing only a snug little tee that bared most of her narrow waist and a pair of bikinis so small and tight they displayed the folds of her pussy.

The woman had pulled out the big guns.

"Would you like me to massage your leg?"

Mac glared, feeling heat fill his cheeks. She'd given a show of consideration he didn't believe for a minute. She'd challenged his manhood with mention of his injury, but shielded her challenge by offering a kindness.

If any other woman had offered, he would have accepted it at face value, but Suki was damn devious. The slight quirk at one corner of her lips gave her away.

He turned, fisting his hands on his hips, and swept her head to toe with a slow, intimate glance. "I was thinking about hitting the shower," he said slowly.

Her eyebrows lowered, and her chest rose on a sharp breath. "Well, I guess I'll just head to bed. Good night." She turned on her heels and stomped down the hallway.

Mac followed, slowing his steps outside the bathroom door, opening and closing it, and then leaned against the frame of her door.

He didn't have to wait long. Her door creaked open, her gaze widening and lifting to meet his. "I was just going to the kitchen," she said, lifting her chin. "For a snack . . . seeing as how you'll be a while."

Mac's smile stretched his lips slowly. "Think we're hungry for the same thing?"

She tossed back her head. "What? You want some pork 'n' beans, too?"

"You got it half right anyway," he murmured. "You always prance around your home half naked?" His glance slid over the front of her tee, snagging on the nipples that beaded under the thin fabric.

Her lips twitched. "I don't prance."

"No, you don't."

Her next inhalation was a little shallow. "My, it's gotten warm in here, don't you think?"

"Maybe."

Suki stepped back and lifted the hem of her tee, pulling it over her head. "That's much better."

Mac sucked in a deep breath, his gaze lowering to her small breasts. Dropping any pretense of taking his time, he shucked his T-shirt and opened his jeans, shoving them down his legs and stepping out of them while she rolled her tiny bikinis down her thighs.

When they were both naked, he eyed the bed. "I want you in the middle of it on your back."

She turned, giving him an eyeful of her sexy little ass as she crawled onto the bed, and then rested on her elbows in the center of the mattress.

Mac crawled on his hands and one good knee until he hovered over her.

With moonlight streaming through the window, he studied her pale, slender body. She was built so slight, he wondered how she'd taken him before. Narrow shoulders, waist, and hips. A concave belly that trembled with her shallow breaths.

Mac swept down to glide his lips over hers. "I finally have you in a bed."

She let out a shaky breath. "Have any idea what you want to do?"

He settled his chest over hers, enjoying the soft jab of her nipples. "I'm pretty sure I'm going to fuck you."

She snorted. "You think? Sure you don't want me to do the work? I mean, I wouldn't want you to hurt yourself."

"Why is it I get the feeling you stopped feeling sorry for me some time today?"

"I stopped worrying about you and your goddamn leg when you paced around the house like a growly bear. If it hurt that damn bad, you would have stopped and had a conversation with me."

"Why do women always wanna talk?"

A fine crease wrinkled her brow as she considered his question. "Maybe because it's a way to connect? When you aren't holding me, I want to know you're still with me."

He hadn't expected such an honest answer. Mac knew her response had taken courage. She'd as much as told him she truly cared about him. "What I'm thinking about matters to you?" She nodded, her expression not giving away everything she felt. "Why?"

The casual lift of her shoulders didn't match the wariness of her expressive eyes. "I like knowing I'm not in this alone."

"I told you I'd stay until this is done."

"I'm not talking about Manny."

Mac exhaled and leaned in to press another kiss against her soft lips. "You mean . . . us. You and me."

Her eyes rolled. "See? It's hard for you to even consider there might be an 'us.' "

"Maybe I've been worrying about the same thing," he growled like the bear she'd accused him of being.

"Sure you have. That's why you couldn't stay far enough away from me all afternoon."

"I had to keep on task. Your safety comes first."

"And after you'd checked the damn doors and windows for the hundredth time, why couldn't you just settle down in a chair and be with me then?"

Mac leaned to one side and then clasped her wrist, drawing her hand down between their bodies until her fingers glided over his cock. "This kinda made conversation between us impossible. If I settled on the sofa for longer than a minute, I'd have pulled you over my lap and fucked you right then."

"I wouldn't have minded," she said flatly.

"As much company as we've had in and out of here today, I didn't want the distraction."

"If you're so worried, why are you here now?"

"I can't fight it anymore. Can't stay away. I've been dying to get you under me so I can sink right inside you, fuck you the way a man does when he's crazy for a woman."

Her eyes narrowed. "You're *crazy* for me?"

"Don't ask me for a definition. I don't know how deep this goes. Not yet."

"All right. I won't push. But maybe I won't let you have everything I have to give either."

Which made him wonder what she would hold back. "This enough for you now?" he asked, holding her gaze with his.

"It's more than I expected. We've known each other only a day. What do we really know about each other?"

"That's right. We've got time to learn more. If you want. . . ."

Suki curled her fingers and stroked his cheek with the backs of her fingers. "We can take it slow."

Mac closed his eyes, enjoying the caress. "Maybe not so slow. Pulling back just might kill me now."

A very feminine smile curved her lips. "Just remember you don't have to be macho with me. If that leg starts to cramp, we can always switch."

"I think I'll manage just fine. I only need one knee to lean on. And there's not a thing wrong with my dick."

6

Suki sucked in a trembling breath. With Mac's weight pressing her into the mattress, her insides had turned to Jell-O. All that heavy muscle tensing above her pretty much took her breath away.

She reached above her head, slipped her hand under her pillow, and came back with a foil packet held between her fingertips.

Mac's slow, wicked smile warmed her to her toes. "We're gonna have to stop at a store tomorrow and get the right size. Those things aren't gonna hold up."

With his chest pressed to hers, every rumbling word vibrated through her. "So long as it stays on just long enough. . . ."

Laughter shook Mac's chest, and his head sank against her shoulder. "Suki . . . baby . . . it'll be a goddamn miracle if I last longer than two seconds."

"Been kinda rough for you today?"

"I'm sorry. The cool water helped some today, but I've been hard all day."

"Just go ahead and do me. I'm sure you'll find a way to make it up to me."

"Promise. Soon as I catch my breath."

Suki raised her knees and cupped his hips as he slipped on the condom and centered his cock between her folds, pushing inside.

Mac's breaths deepened, his eyes closed, and the look that crossed his face was worth any pleasure she might have to forestall for the moment.

He looked as if he'd stolen into heaven. His mouth opened around a silent moan. He took several tentative strokes, gliding in the cream her body released, and then pumped furiously. Quickly his soft grunts grew more strained. His jaw tightened. His head ducked closer to his chest.

She knew the moment he came because his whole body shuddered and jerked as he thrust hard and a long, whispering groan erupted from him.

Suki held him as his motions slowed. She smoothed her hands up and down his sweaty back, providing what comfort she could as he gasped and trembled above her.

When his eyes opened, a crooked grin curved his firm lips. "Guess two seconds was overconfidence."

Suki bracketed his face and reached up to kiss him. "I don't mind. Really."

"Gimme a minute."

She kissed his cheek, his chin, and then pulled his face down to rest beside hers. "I'll give you two."

"Uh . . . think this rubber's had it." He groaned and withdrew from her, rolling off her to lie on his back.

Suki missed his weight but rolled to her side, resting her head on a hand as she watched him slide off the condom.

"Hate these things." He jackknifed upward to sit at the side of the bed and got up.

She watched him walk from the room, heard him close the bathroom door across the hallway, and then slumped against the mattress, feeling deliciously relaxed, if still more than a little aroused.

"No, you don't," he chided when he returned.

She opened her eyes. "I wasn't sleeping."

He sat beside her on the bed, curving his palm around the corner of her shoulder, and then leaned down to kiss her.

Her lips opened for him, accepting the gentle thrust of his tongue. She sighed and slid her tongue alongside his, sharing a lazy kiss that quickly grew more heated.

When they broke apart, they both breathed hard.

Mac stretched out beside her on the bed, scooting down until his face was level with her breasts. His thumb and fingers surrounded her uppermost curve and gave her a caress.

She sighed and settled her head deeper on her palm, content to watch him.

"I love your tits."

A wide grin stretched her lips. " *'Tits'!* Don't you know girls hate that word?"

"You do? I love it. 'Breasts' gets hard to enunciate when a man's turned on."

She arched a brow. "You just came, so what's your excuse?"

"I wanted to shock you."

"You'll have to work a little harder to do that."

A smile played at the corners of his lips. "I'm gettin' there. Your tits are pretty, by the way."

"Really? I always thought they were kinda small."

"I like brown nipples. And yours are shiny and smooth. Not bumpy."

"Save for one prominent bump."

His tongue fluttered against her "bump." Then he released a loud sigh. "Not winning any prizes for compliments, am I?"

"It's not what you say that's gonna win you medals, soldier boy." She caressed the back of his head, urging him closer. "I like this."

"What?" he murmured, licking the underside of her breast.

"No rush. You playful. Feels like we've done this before."

"Promise, I would have remembered."

She punched him. "You know what I mean."

"Yeah. It's . . . comfortable. And something I hope we do often."

"You don't see me objecting," she said breathlessly.

His thumb rasped the sensitive tip.

Suki sucked in deep breath. "Maybe not so comfortable after all."

"Too sensitive?"

"No, just right. Felt that all the way to my toes."

"Lie back, sweetheart. Let me do this right."

Suki rolled to her back and groaned as his mouth followed, suckling at her "tit." Wet heat surrounded her breast. His mouth tugged and nipped until her legs shifted restlessly on the bed and sighs broke from between her bitten lips. "The other one?"

His mouth came off her breast with an audible *pop* and then trailed to other breast. His lips drew on the tip, tugging side to side, driving her knees upward as an electric pulse shot straight toward her womb.

Mac smoothed a hand down her belly, combed his fingers through her curls, and then sank one between her folds.

"God, you're wet," he growled against her skin.

221

"You make me that way." She pulled on his ears, trying to direct him lower.

His laughter gusted against her wet nipple.

She tugged harder until, at last, he scooted down the bed, leaving a moist trail of kisses down her quivering belly.

When he settled on his elbows between her legs, she reached for the pillow above her and shoved it under her head. No way was she going to miss a thing.

His gaze gleamed in the moonlight filtering through the curtains, and then he bent toward her sex. His fingers spread her folds, and he dove down to lap along the furled edges of her inner lips.

Suki threaded her fingers through his hair, offering unspoken praise for his efforts while her other hand caressed her breast, keeping the nipple warmed and primed.

Mac pinched the hood cloaking her clit and pushed it back, exposing her clit to his warm breath and the stroke of his hot tongue.

Her fingers tightened, pulling at his hair, plucking her nipple, and her hips began to dance, rising to meet his wicked mouth.

He thrust two fingers inside her, swirling in the honey her body oozed. He pulled them out and licked them, sucking them into his mouth as she watched, his eyes closing as though he tasted ambrosia. Then he rimmed her opening, drawing more cream, and slid lower, painting a wet path as he dragged his fingertips down to her back entrance.

Suki's breath hitched. Her heart thudded hard against her ribs.

As he circled her small opening, she held her hips still, held her breath, and then groaned as he pressed inside, slipping past the tight ring.

His thumb entered her vagina, and he stroked both fingers in and out and then closed his lips around her clit to suckle it.

Tension spiked deep inside her womb, and she slammed her hips upward, unable to control her movements as her orgasm swept over her in delicious waves of heat. Goose bumps dimpled her skin, and she squeezed her eyes closed as lights burst behind her lids.

His strokes deepened. His mouth drew endlessly on her clit until at last her hips trembled and rested against the mattress.

Suki came back to herself, noting the broad strokes of his tongue lapping at the liquid spilling from inside her. She straightened her legs and lifted her arms above her head. "Mac . . ." she breathed.

He climbed up her body and settled on top of her, stretching to cover her from chest to curling toes. "Did I make up for leaving you behind?"

Without opening her eyes, she grinned. "You've killed me. I'm totally boneless."

"I take it that's a good thing?"

She slowly opened her eyes, taking in the small, satisfied smile that curved his firm lips. "You know it was good. Do you need praise?"

"If that smile's anything to go by, I did all right."

"Better than all right." She breathed deeply, dragging in the scent of sex. When his hands reached up to hold hers, she squeezed them. "I've never had it this good. This intense."

"Baby, I haven't even gotten started."

Soft laughter shook her chest. Her eyelids drifted closed and then opened drowsily. "Think you've worn me out."

Mac's smile deepened, and then he rolled off her. "Snuggle your back against me. I'll hold you while you sleep."

Suki settled close, her head resting on his shoulder. She

loved the way his arms enfolded her, and she slid hers over his, hugging him back. "Wake me in a while?"

"Sleep, baby," he whispered and then kissed the rim of her ear.

With his breaths deepening behind her, she closed her eyes and fell blissfully asleep.

Mac came awake in the darkness, not sure what had pulled him from the first deep sleep he'd enjoyed in a long time that wasn't drug or alcohol induced.

Lying beside Suki, he concentrated on the sounds around him—Suki's quiet breathing, the wind outside sifting through the trees, a limb scraping the side of the house. Nothing out of the ordinary.

However, now that he was wide awake, he decided to make another round of checks.

Tomorrow they'd sleep under his roof. He'd make arrangements for the ranch hands to take shifts to provide him relief and the opportunity to relax a bit with Suki, maybe deepen the slender threads of affection beginning to bind them closer.

Maybe he'd even try to sit on a horse.

It felt like forever since the last ride he'd taken before he'd shipped out. He'd wanted to be alone, slipping away from Lyssa, who'd wanted to remain close in those last days. She hadn't understood his need to surround himself with quiet.

While she'd wanted to fill their days with memories to hold close over the coming months, he'd wanted to empty his heart and mind—go a little numb.

As much as he believed in what he had to do and never questioned his commitment to go with the men he'd trained with for years, still he'd needed to leave a part of himself behind on the wide-open plain.

Always self-reliant, he'd had to submerge the cowboy to be

a part of a team. He hoped now he could find the part of himself he'd shed. He wanted to rejoin his old life, reconnect with his sister and his friends, and slowly rebuild his relationship with the land he'd loved since he'd taken his first steps across a dusty corral.

Then maybe he'd feel like he was man enough to be with a woman like Suki.

She deserved someone whole, someone who didn't flinch at noises, didn't grit his teeth against pain when he made love.

He pulled on his jeans, dug through his duffel for a pack of smokes, and made his way through the house, tilting his head to the side as he strained to listen.

He turned off the porch light and stepped outside, lit his cigarette, and dragged nicotine deep into his lungs.

One last crutch he'd have to discard if he was serious about pursuing Suki. But, for now, he enjoyed the pleasant buzz and leaned forward against the porch rail to stare up into the starry sky.

A heavy footstep trod the planks behind him.

Mac grew rigid but calmly lifted his cigarette up for another draw. Whoever it was, Mac couldn't outmaneuver him. He just wasn't quick enough. And he hadn't touched the Glock since surrendering it to Suki. Hadn't seen or heard a hint of danger . . . until now.

Beneath his feet, he felt the subtle shift of the boards as someone stepped closer.

Mac dropped the cigarette, pivoted on his good foot, and drew back his fist.

Moonlight glinted on a long, cylindrical object just before it jabbed at his belly, forcing him to double over against the pain and the sudden loss of air.

Mac opened his arms and plowed forward, taking his assailant to the floor.

As they fell, Mac knew instantly he didn't have a hope in hell of besting the man in a fair fight. Even without the heavy metal pipe Manny used to pummel his back and leg, the man was heavy, built like a goddamn rock.

His only hope of survival was making enough noise to rouse Suki from her sleep. If she could get to her gun, she might save herself.

Digging deep for the strength inside him, Mac reached for the arm wielding the pipe and crashed the other man's knuckles against the porch.

Manny pummeled his side with his fist, bucked his knees and thighs, hitting Mac squarely in his injured leg.

Pain sliced through Mac, taking away his breath, giving Manny the advantage. Manny rolled them, coming up on top of Mac, the pipe pressing hard against Mac's windpipe.

Mac fought for breath, shoved at the pipe, straining his arms and chest to get it off before he passed out. Slowly he pressed it upward, his arms burning and trembling with the effort. He sucked in a deep breath. "Suki!"

Manny's lips drew back from his teeth. He pulled the pipe away from Mac's grasp and lifted it above his head.

Mac raised his forearm to prepare for the blow, but an explosion ripped the air; gunpowder flashed.

Manny slumped forward, the pipe rolling away from his limp fingers.

Mac shoved him off, rolled to his good knee, and glanced up.

Suki stood nude in the doorway, the barrel of her shotgun sagging toward the ground.

Mac reached up to take it from her, spared only a glance at Manny to make sure he hadn't moved, and then reached out an arm to snag Suki's waist and draw her close.

He sank his head against her trembling belly, gave her a quick, fierce kiss, and then pulled himself up her body.

She trembled, but her knees locked. As soon as he stood in front of her, she launched herself into his arms.

Mac held her close, swaying on his feet as his chest billowed, drawing air deep into his lungs. His heartbeats slowed, as did the shudders that racked his body. He kissed the top of her head, which was buried against his chest. "You did good, sweetheart. You saved us both."

A soft sob shook her body. "I was so scared," she whispered.

"Shhh . . . it's over. We're both safe now," he crooned as his hands glided up and down her bare back.

The blare of a siren sounded from the highway, slowing as the vehicle turned onto the gravel road.

"Think you can help me inside?" he asked softly.

Her head shook. "Can't move. My knees are shaking too bad."

"We're about to have some company."

"Don't care."

Mac's lips curved up. As soon as she realized she was buck naked, she'd care, all right. But he'd kill any man who raised an eyebrow.

As the blue lights strobed closer, he turned to shield her slim body from their glare.

She whimpered and drew a ragged, indrawn breath. "I was afraid I'd hit you. . . . Wasn't sure which one was on top until he raised the pipe. . . . Saw it shining in his hand. Knew it couldn't be you."

"I'm glad you waited for a clear shot," he murmured.

Footsteps crunched on the gravel path beside the house. "McDonough, you and the lady okay?"

Mac aimed a glare over his shoulder. "Nothing more than a few bruises here."

A deputy ran up the steps and knelt beside Manny. "This one's gonna need the coroner. Sure you don't need EMTs?"

Mac shook his head. "No."

"He hit you!" Suki cried.

"I'll survive it. Had worse getting kicked by my horse."

The deputy gave Suki a quick glance and then headed into the house. A few moments later, he returned with a blanket and wrapped it around her shoulders. "We're about to have company," he said softly, his gaze meeting Mac's.

"She knows."

"You two want to come inside and have a seat?"

"Suki," Mac whispered, "can you make it inside now?"

She nodded against his chest but didn't move away.

Mac wished like hell he could carry her, but even without bruised ribs he knew he wouldn't manage. "Deputy, can you take her?"

The deputy stepped close, and Mac pried her fingers from his shoulders. She melted against the other man, but her eyes never left Mac's face.

"Just to the couch," Mac said, not liking how pale her features had become. "I'll get her some clothes."

"You sit. I'll find her something to put on."

Mac sat on the sofa and accepted Suki's weight on his lap while the deputy strode toward the bedroom.

"Can we leave tonight?" she asked quietly.

"I'll give Tara a call. We'll need someone else to drive. My leg's screaming, and you're in no condition."

Outside more vehicles arrived as Mac quietly dressed Suki. Soon the house was filled with law officers.

Through it all, Mac sat holding Suki close against his chest.

He answered their questions in an even voice, not letting them badger Suki, who kept her face pressed against his skin.

When two familiar faces appeared in the doorway, he wasn't surprised.

Brand strode quickly inside and knelt beside them. "I'll take her, Mac."

Mac realized he might have gone a little into shock when Brand had to repeat his words before he understood. Reluctantly he let his friend lift Suki into his arms.

As he strode away, Lyssa entered his sight, kneeling in front of him, her eyes glittering with unshed tears. "Think you can make it to the car on your own?"

Mac swallowed, never having been so glad to see her beautiful face. "I can if you let me lean on your shoulder."

Lyssa gave him a blinding smile. "Are you saying you need my help?"

Mac gave her a crooked smile and pushed up from his seat. "I suppose you're not going to let me forget it."

"Damn straight." She wrapped her arm around his waist and gave him a squeeze.

Air hissed between clenched teeth.

Her arm loosened instantly. "Damnit, you're hurt."

"Just get me to the car—and don't try kissin' me, or you'll kill me."

Lyssa's eyes flashed green fire. "You know there's not a chance in hell we aren't taking you to an emergency room."

"Lyss, I just want to get Suki someplace quiet. I don't want her upset any more than she already is."

"Can I at least call a doctor?"

Mac rolled his eyes and took a step forward, forcing her to follow. "Anyone ever tell you you're stubborn as a damn mule?"

"Dear Jesus, do I have to hear it from both of you now?"

He snorted, feeling blood surge through his body again, renewing his strength and clearing his mind. "You mean Brand noticed?"

"Does he ever shut up about it?"

He clucked. "Always thought he was the quiet type."

"He is—except when he's lighting into me."

"Are you blushing?" he asked, cocking his head to the side to get a better look at her bright, glowing face.

"Just drop it," she said flatly.

"Looks like I'm gonna have to have a talk with Brand."

"Don't you dare."

Mac chuckled softly next to her, grateful for her light banter. The tension in her jaw, and the soft trembling in her frame as she helped him outside, told him what it cost her.

"Sis, I'm glad you're here."

"Where else would I be, Mac?"

Indeed, she'd never abandoned him. Even when he'd begged her to.

As they approached Tara's silver SUV, Mac caught a glimpse of Suki's pale face in the backseat window. "You're gonna have to help me sit on this one, Lyss."

"You mean there's a girl out there who's immune to the McDonough charm?"

"What charm?"

"Damn, you sound just like Brand." Lyssa halted when he did, and her glance went to the vehicle. "She mean that much to you?"

"I think she's gonna be my whole world."

Lyssa's head snuggled against his chest. "I'll tie her down with duct tape if it comes to that."

Laughter made him wince. "Something a little more subtle, please."

"Subtle's my middle name."

Epilogue

Sunlight rimmed the edge of the horizon in a brilliant show of red and orange, fading to mauve as the nighttime sky pressed downward. A crescent moon hovered overhead while seven tired riders pointed their horses toward home.

"Did you enjoy today?" Mac murmured behind her.

Suki leaned back against his rock-hard chest and sighed. "Still think you should have let me ride my own horse."

"When you've got a little more experience. For now, just let me do the driving." Mac held the reins with one hand, the other snuggled against her belly. Every now and then, his thumb swept upward to nudge the underside of her breast—like now.

She placed her hand over his. "I'm going to need a long soak."

"A little saddle sore?" he whispered.

"Uh-huh."

"I have some cream. . . ."

She chuckled, remembering the first time he'd tended her tender spots.

"You won't have to move a muscle. Just lie there and let me do all the work."

"Stop with the whispers!" Lyssa called out. "I can hear, you know. You're my brother, for Pete's sake." She gave a mock shudder. "Blech!"

Soft laughter sifted among the male riders. Glances were shared.

Suki understood their sign language by now. The men were horny as hell.

"This is so goddamn unfair," Tara said.

"You had your chance," Mac said cheerfully.

"Yeah, I know. But you're not my type, no matter how well you fill a pair of jeans, soldier boy."

Suki felt her face heat as the other three women shot her knowing glances and smiled.

Suki wasn't the only woman sharing a mount. Maggie sat in front of Danny on the gentlest mare he could find.

"How's your stomach?" Danny asked, his hand gliding over the gentle mound.

"Supper's staying down, for now."

"We're almost home. Maybe Mac will lend us some of that cream. . . ."

She elbowed him. "Behave yourself, husband."

"Why? You love it when I'm bad," he said with a silky slide of his voice.

Lyssa reined in next to Tara. "You still got a hankering for that badass cowboy?"

"Maybe," Tara said, her lips tightening.

"We need to make a plan."

A soft curse burst from Brand. "Woman, only plans you should be makin' are for our wedding."

"Thought you weren't in any all-fired hurry, cowboy. It's not like you're waitin' to get a thing."

"Hush, you're brother's listening. One day he's gonna decide it's time to kick my ass."

Mac grunted, and Suki didn't need to glance behind her to know his gaze narrowed on his best friend.

Lights from the McDonough ranch house beckoned them closer.

Brand spurred his horse ahead. Lyssa clucked at her horse and kept right on the tail of his horse. They pulled back their reins next to the front porch, dismounted, and wrapped the reins around the rail.

Brand grabbed her hand and pulled her close, bending her over his arm for a deep kiss as the rest of the group pulled up.

"Jesus, can't you wait until you're out of sight?" Mac grumbled, though his chest shook. "That's my sister you're molesting."

Brand raised Lyssa and slid an arm around her waist. "Coffee. Then we're headin' out."

Everyone gathered in the kitchen in pairs, except Tara, who bustled around the room as if it were hers, serving up steaming mugs before settling on a chair next to Lyssa.

Tara wrapped her hands around her cup and sighed deeply. "Guess I'm not needed here anymore. I have a bar to run, tourists to entertain, and cowboys to keep out of trouble."

Suki felt a jolt of alarm. With the other two couples leaving that night, it meant she'd be alone with Mac.

While the thought raised prickles of awareness all over her body, she knew the time drew near when she'd have to leave as well.

Tara stood and stretched her hands above her head. "Damn, my ass is sore."

Chuckles drifted lazily around the room as she bent and gave Mac a quick kiss on his cheek. "Don't screw it up," she whispered overloud.

Mac grimaced and gave her bottom a swat. "Mind your own damn business."

She stopped in front of Suki and opened her arms. Suki stood and gave her a hug.

Tara's eyebrows bobbed in a wicked waggle. "Go easy on my boy."

Suki felt the heat enter her cheeks and refused to meet Mac's amused glance. "Have a nice drive back to town," she murmured.

"That a euphemism for 'get the hell out'?"

Suki didn't answer, biting back a grin as Tara flipped her hair behind her shoulders. "Don't be a stranger."

"Don't think that woman ever met one," Danny muttered. Danny pulled Maggie onto his knee and wrapped his arms around the slight swell of her belly. "Think we'll head out, too. Want to get home before it gets too late. This one needs her beauty sleep."

Maggie pushed his hands off her belly. "Can't you wait to start fondling me until we're alone?"

"Wouldn't be as much fun."

Maggie pushed off Danny's knee and came around the table to give Mac a quick kiss. "We're glad you're back."

Mac held her hand. "I'm glad Danny found you. Haven't ever seen him so happy."

After Danny and Maggie made the rounds of hugs and kisses, Brand and Lyssa shared a charged glance and started to rise. "Guess we're gonna head back home."

Mac's gaze rested on his sister. "I've been thinking."

"About?"

"Guess I won't kick Brand's ass after all."

Lyssa laughed. "Had to think about that one, did you?"

"Well, it would be a few months before I could win, and I think I like the way you two look together. Make a nice couple."

Lyssa smiled blissfully. "We do, don't we?"

"Besides, Danny says Brand knows just how to keep you out of trouble."

Lyssa's green eyes sparkled with outrage. "He didn't tell you, did he?"

Mac winked at Brand. "A firm hand . . ."

Brand's lips stretched wide. "Does the trick, all right."

Lyssa screeched in mock outrage and then launched herself at Brand, wrapping her arms around his waist. "I don't think I'll be back for at least a week, big brother. It'll take that long to lose the blush."

Mac rose to his feet with more grace than he would have managed just a week ago and wrapped his arms around his sister. "I love you, Lyss."

Lyssa hugged him back. "I love you, too. I'm so glad you're back."

"Sorry I cussed you out."

"You weren't yourself."

He sighed and hugged her hard. "I don't want to meet that other man again."

As Lyssa and Brand said their farewells to Suki, Mac settled back against the counter.

When the couple trailed out of the room, Suki let out a deep breath and faced him. "It's just us now."

"Yeah. Gonna be quiet."

"Think so?" she asked, fishing for a clue about how he really felt. With all the company, they hadn't really had time to talk.

"Quiet, punctuated with moments of heavy breathing. . . ."

Her lips twitched. "And a lot of inappropriate religious references. . . ."

Mac gave her a sly grin. "Could get kinda loud. Don't think I can make it to the bedroom."

"Is your leg bothering you?"

Mac shook his head.

Suki took a deep breath and came closer, close enough that he grabbed her by the waist and settled her bottom on top of the kitchen table.

"Imagine that—just the right height," he murmured, rubbing his crotch against the juncture of her thighs.

"Good thing we're all alone," she said breathlessly. "This could get embarrassing awfully fast."

Mac made quick work of her shorts, stripping them down her thighs. Then he raised her again to sit on the edge of the table and removed her shirt.

When she reached for his clothing, Mac pushed her hands away, unzipped his pants, and shoved them down his hips. Then he leaned close as he held himself and rubbed his cock along her slick seam.

"Damn," he breathed, "Feels fucking incredible."

Suki couldn't agree more but kept silent as she enjoyed the sexy glides. They needed to talk. And soon. Her heart couldn't take another day of uncertainty.

Mac placed himself at her entrance and slipped an inch inside, punching forward, drawing back, teasing her with glimpses of the blunt pressure he'd exert once he slipped inside.

He paused, and his gaze locked with hers. "Baby, I'm gonna keep you so busy, so full, you're not gonna have time to think about that other life you had. The one before you knew me."

Suki dragged in a ragged breath. *He chooses now to let me*

know? "It wasn't all that great," she said, smiling through her tears, fighting to keep focused on the conversation while his cock pulsed impatiently between her folds.

"I traveled a lot, met some interesting people, but I always had this secret hankering for a soldier boy in a cowboy hat. Know anyone like that?"

His lop-sided smile held a hint of doubt. "I just might. But he's a little bit beat up."

Suki reached up to cup his cheek. "He's strong and brave— and absolutely perfect. . . ." She ran a finger down the scar on his cheek. "And so handsome he takes my breath away."

Mac's strong hips flexed, and he sank deep into her body, his powerful frame shuddering. "Don't think I can ever get enough of this," he said between clenched teeth. "Didn't know this was what was missing from my life."

She gasped, and her back arched, but her gaze didn't waver for a second from his. "What were you missing, Mac? A willing woman to slide up inside?"

Mac's expression grew solemn. "You're so much more than that. Hope it's that way for you, too. I'd hate to be here alone."

Suki spread her arms wide and clutched the edges of the table. Joy burst through her, making her fearless at last. "You fill me. In every way possible. I love you, Mac McDonough."

As he began to stroke firmly in and out of her warm, wet passage, Mac ran his palms over her soft belly, bent, and kissed her small, dark nipples, lingering long enough to draw the tips into tightly beading points.

With her almond-shaped eyes glistening with moisture, her lush lips trembling, he knew she waited for him to declare his love. Thank God, he was finally ready. He felt strong, nearly healed, completely whole. All because of her.

The words, once so impossible to imagine, rushed out of him in a grateful flurry as every muscle in his body tensed. "I love you, Suki," he said, his voice tightening against the emotions roiling inside him. "I love you, baby. I'll never let you go."

His arms swept under her knees and pulled her bottom to the edge of the table. Then words were truly impossible as he powered into her, hammering at her pussy, losing his mind in the sweetest way when her moans floated in the air around him.

When he'd spent the last of his strength and seed inside her, he pulled her up, grabbed her small, round ass, and hefted her off the table. His cock still locked deep inside her juicy cunt, he walked slowly through the house.

"What about your leg?" she asked as she peppered his face and neck with kisses.

"Bet it'll hurt like hell tomorrow," he said, smiling because he didn't give a damn.

"God, Mac!" she groaned. "You don't know how good this feels. Each step . . . *Jesus!*"

Feeling like a man, a better one than had left the ranch so many months ago, Mac cuddled her close and strode toward the bedroom. Though horrors might still visit him from time to time in dreams, all his waking life would be sweet, filled with the warmth of his family's love.

Suki would be family as soon as he could pry himself from his bed—maybe after a week or two, when they were both so raw and well used they might need the break to recuperate.

"What are you smiling about?" she asked as he came over her on the mattress.

He kissed her mouth. "I'm happy."

Her pleased smile flashed white in the gathering darkness. "How about we lock the doors and turn off all the lights? Maybe everyone will think we've escaped."

"I like the way you think," he said, sliding his cheek alongside hers as he began to rut gently against her.

Suki widened her legs and cupped her hips to aid his entry. "We could always borrow the keys to Tara's cabin. . . ."

"Too far," he said, centering his semisoft cock between her legs and forcing himself inside. "You're going to have to help me, here."

"Need some encouragement?" she drawled and squeezed her inner muscles around him.

Mac grunted. "Do that a while, and I think he'll perk right up." Already, miraculously, he felt his cock surge and fill, nudging northward.

"Have I told you how much I love your dick?"

"Suki!" He jerked back his head, frowning in disapproval. "Don't you know how much guys hate to hear that word come out of a woman's mouth?"

She shrugged, seemingly unconcerned. "It's what you call it."

"I do n—okay, you've got me there."

Her eyes narrowed. "You like tits, I like dick."

"We're gonna have to build a better vocabulary," he growled.

"Maybe we could start with . . ." She raised her head to whisper in his ear.

Mac felt heat scorch his cheeks as bone-deep pleasure filled him with her playfulness. "That's not really a word. It's a number."

Suki rolled her eyes, but her delighted grin said how much she loved surprising him.

Mac felt a grin tug his lips. Then he bent and swept her lips with a kiss, trying to tell her without words just how much he loved her.

Her lips melted beneath his; her fingers dug into his shoulders. When they drew apart, they shared smiles filled with silent promises.

"Lady's choice," he whispered, sipping at her mouth. "Whenever you're ready, just say the word."

Suki's lips curved beneath his into a sweet, satisfied smile. "It's a number."